"I ask that if you find anything edifying, anything consoling, anything well presented, that you give all praise, all glory and all honor to the Blessed Son of God Jesus Christ. If on the other hand, you find anything that is ill composed, uninteresting or not too well explained you impute and attribute it to my weakness, blindness and lack of skill."

Saint Anthony of Padua, *Sermones*

1

TUESDAY, APRIL 4

They were about 40 steps from the elevator. The girl had to add little skips every few paces to match her grandfather's stride. With one of the skips, she inched ahead of him. She glanced up and smirked. He lengthened his stride, took the lead, and smirked back. She threw a bony shoulder into his hip and accelerated to a speed-walk.

Joe Brescia, the founder and CEO of Brescia Global Solutions and his eleven-year-old granddaughter, Juliana, had not planned to race-walk from his office to the elevator but here they were. Little games and challenges sprung up whenever they were together. This was the end of her weekly visit to his company's Midtown headquarters. Her father waited for them in the lobby, 38 floors below.

They moved stiffly and briskly down the executive corridor – like a pair of ostriches or amateurs on stilts. About 25 steps remained in the wood-paneled and conference room-lined hallway. She giggled and pushed the pace. The key was to move quickly but not look like you were the one who was racing.

Both abandoned the pretense of walking as the carpet changed to marble and the elevator came within reach. Juliana touched it an instant before he did. Joe's pace had mysteriously and discretely slowed at the last moment. Juliana celebrated her victory with a little fist pump and a littler hoot. She was unsure of the proper post-race etiquette, so after a pause, she extended her hand. He shook it with congratulatory deference, proud more that she was gracious than that she was fast.

"Good race, Pop."

"Thank you, Miss. That was a close one."

She hugged his waist and remained there, pressed into his side. His arm reflexively found its way around her shoulder and then they were no longer competitors but Poppy and Miss, grandfather and granddaughter.

They caught sight of their reflection in the chrome door, fun-house caricatures of themselves. It showed Juliana with a few of her recent firsts. The lip gloss started a few weeks back. She toted a little pocketbook now, too. The ponytail was gone, replaced by something trendy which Joe had described as a "side sweep." Dark glasses, dark eyebrows, bright mouth. A toothy smile awaited braces.

They made silly faces at each other. Squadrons of gray invaders had conquered most of Joe's sideburns and temple but were unable to advance significantly into blacker territories. There was the considerable Roman nose his father and grandfather had also worn. Martini olive-green eyes peered from under a hairline that, at 63, still refused to yield to time's insistence on receding.

Juliana pressed the arrow pointing down and an elevator cab hustled to oblige.

Behind them, a young woman in a dark suit stepped out of a conference room. She lingered behind a rubber tree plant, observing them. Long red hair – dark like pinot noir and pouring down like it, too – was pulled forward over one shoulder. She possessed restless eyes; always scanning, gauging, assessing. A thin frown. Arms folded across her blouse. She waited until Joe's glance found hers. When it did, she lifted her eyebrows and jutted her chin.

Joe reached down and took Juliana's hand.

The girl stood up on her tiptoes, trying to balance on them. She lasted six seconds.

"How many questions do you think I can get this time?" Juliana asked, bringing her grandfather back from whatever place he had just gone to in his mind.

"What's your record?"

"Hmm. I think I had seven last week."

"No, Miss. You had four." He feigned a frown.

"No way!" she squealed. "I had at least seven."

"I'm pretty sure it was four. I was there."

"So was I. It was seven! What do I get if I win this week?"

Joe smiled and narrowed his brow, both curious and skeptical. "What are your terms?"

"If I get seven, will you tell my dad to get me a cell phone?"

Joe clutched his chest and asked the heavens how his little Miss had gotten so big so fast.

The elevator doors opened and Joe and Juliana stepped in. As they closed, a hand flitted in and the doors pushed back. The young woman in the dark suit eased into the elevator languidly, like spilled wine crawling on a tablecloth. Her eyes locked onto Joe's. She didn't turn around to press a button.

"Mr. Brescia." She had a breathy, sighing way of speaking. It sounded like everything was either unbearably boring or unbearably desirable.

He regarded her coolly, an extra moment passing.

"Tori. Hi."

"Who's the little one?" She didn't look at Juliana.

"She's my granddaughter," Joe said, shifting his frame between her and the child.

The elevator walls crept toward each other. Tori tilted her head, scanned his face. He tried to hold her gaze. Just as the moment was about to become something, Tori knelt. She leaned in close to Juliana, her hand brushing Joe's belt buckle as she reached out to cup the girl's face.

"Well, look how beautiful you are. My name's Tori."

"Hi. Uhh, thank you. You're really pretty too. I love your red hair. It's *so* red."

"Why, thank you. Juliana, is it? I bet your grandpa thinks we're both really pretty, right?" She stood back up as she said it, more to him than to her.

Juliana wasn't sure how to respond so she made a noise that sounded like a laugh and looked up at her grandfather. He seemed so serious.

"Poppy, are you ready?"

"Ready for what, darling?"

"To play the game. Our elevator game?"

"I'm ready," he shifted his shoulders toward Juliana.

"What's the game?" Tori asked brightly.

"I have until the elevator gets to the bottom to answer as many questions as possible. It goes by really quick. You can be the scorekeeper if you want." Then she added: "my record's seven." Juliana pressed LOBBY and the elevator began to descend.

"What is the capital of New York?"

"Albany."

"Correct. Who was the second president of the United States?"

"Thomas Jefferson, no, uh, John Adams."

"I'll give it to you." Tori held up two fingers. Her eyes invited Joe's to come back to hers.

"Name three countries that start with the letter 'I'."

"Iraq. Italy. . . I . . .uhhhh . . .I, I, I."

A polite ding ended the game and the doors opened. Tori leaned down and hugged Juliana.

"Take real good care of your grandpa for us, ok?" It wasn't quite a whisper. Then: "Mr. Brescia."

Joe pulled in a breath through his nose and nodded. He and Juliana got off. Tori stayed on the elevator, eyes taking them in as the doors closed again.

The lobby was nearly empty. Their steps clicked in the unfilled space. Two security guards behind the welcome desk stood to acknowledge Joe. He greeted them by name. The men beamed and sat down.

"Who was that lady, Pop?"

"She works for me. Did she make you uncomfortable?"

"Not really.

Juliana's next question was cut off as she caught sight of her father on the other side of the lobby. Her footsteps plinked as she ran to her dad.

Joe's only child, Michael, sat on a leather couch. Elbows on his knees. Tugging at the knot of his tie. He stood with some effort and then stooped to scoop her up. Child in one arm, he hugged his father with the other.

Joe knew better than to ask what was bothering his son. Michael was a city prosecutor. Bouts of insomnia plagued him when he was preparing a difficult case.

"How are you, Dad?" Michael forced a smile.

"Good, Mikey, I'm good. I don't suppose I could convince you to relax a little bit?"

"Actually, Val and I are gonna go to the house for the weekend. You and Mom want to come? We might even bring this one." He winked at his daughter.

Michael meant the family beach house in Connecticut. It was a roomy bungalow on the water in New Haven. Joe and his wife Angela had surprised everyone by giving it to Michael and Valerie as their wedding present.

Joe said "we're in" before Michael finished speaking. He loved when his family was together at the beach house: sitting around the table – laughing, telling stories, tossing and evading wisecracks. A huge *'scalabash* of spaghetti boiling on the stove. Olives plucked sneakily from the salad bowl. Bread and butter. Salt and pepper.

Juliana piped up. "I'm *realllllly* excited, Poppy. I love the beach."

"Me too, Miss." They made plans to meet in New Haven on Saturday morning.

"How's Val doing?" Joe asked his son. Michael's wife was eight months pregnant. Juliana's fervent prayer to be an older sister would soon be answered.

"She's fine. We're almost there."

They shared another round of embraces. Michael and Juliana exited the lobby and got in the back of a waiting sedan. Juliana blew Joe a kiss. The car pulled away and dissolved into the blur of the city.

Coal-colored clouds assembled overhead and choked the last of the daylight. Then they emptied themselves vehemently onto the streets of New York City.

2

THE TIME BEFORE TIME

Lucifer examined the angel in front of him and sighed. It was no one important. Just an energetic Principality waiting his turn like everyone else. The smaller angel bowed politely to Lucifer, who scoffed. A pair of Dominions further ahead throbbed as the line shuffled forward, their colors rippling and blending and bleeding back and forth between them.

When the angels came to the Throne Room to worship, they waited patiently in a line so that each could have a little moment alone with God. This wasn't necessary, of course. God is infinite. The line had been born of charity, not necessity - one of the many ancient customs and traditions of Heaven. The legend went that in the beginning when the angels were created and came to worship God for the first time, each insisted that the other have the first experience. They agreed to take turns and the line to behold his face began. The angels have been doing it ever since.

The unnecessary line in the Throne Room was also where most angels socialized with friends from different Choirs. There was always buzzing and shouting and shimmering, colors leaping back and forth between pairs and groups. (Angels share colors the way humans share words. Angels can speak, and often do, but the colors are just so much more beautiful.) The line also happened to wind past the Light Bearer's post - closer to the Throne Room door than the Throne itself, but still closer than anyone else.

In the beginning, when the Lord God first assigned him to be the Light Bearer and named him for that task, Lucifer performed his duties with such careful reverence. How nobly he guarded the Light! How zealously he stood at attention beside it! *Thank you, My God, thank you*, Lucifer whispered again and again.

But that was all a long time ago.

Over the millennia, the line grew longer and stretched toward his post. The angels waiting in front of him would nod to Lucifer and bow to venerate the Light. And after eons of this, those two gestures became blurry to Lucifer. And one day, he chose to forget the difference. There was a distinct moment, that first time he accepted the praise meant for God. The pride instantly pushed through him, ripped through him, tore through him. It was awful and hot and exhilarating. He felt something like sick. And when it had settled inside him, he was different. Lucifer knew what he was doing was wrong. He hated it, knew what the pride would cost him, knew it with absolute certainty.

But Lucifer wanted to taste it again.

And he knew God could see all of it, as it was happening. He often wondered why God didn't say anything at first. But over the many eons, he stopped wondering. The pride surged through him each time he accepted their salute as if it were his own. But eventually the rush began to dull. He needed bigger and bigger hits. So he made himself more important in his mind. The angels waiting in line in front of his post were there to honor him. And if there wasn't a Seraphim or a Cherubim in front of him, he put on his most bored expression and leaned on the Light, looking down the line for someone important.

He was wondering if *The Bearer of the Light* sounded more majestic and powerful than plain old *Light Bearer* when God spoke. The Living God instructed all the angels to leave the Throne Room, except for Lucifer.

Lucifer advanced to the Throne and prostrated himself before the Father and the Son and the Holy Spirit – the One God. Even after all this time, was still astounded when he could see up close how the One God is Three Divine Persons and the Three Persons are the One God.

When Lucifer stood, the Divine Persons revealed to him, each in their own way, that they would soon fashion a new creature. One made in God's own image and likeness. Lucifer's first thought had been: *More of an image of God than me?*

God explained that the new creatures would be spiritual beings but, unlike the angels, they would also have a physical, bodily existence. They would not have perfect intellects like the angels but they would have rationality and free will. They would be something different: both soul and body. Furthermore, these beings would be the privileged recipients of God's love and attention.

Lucifer tried to hide his disgust but he knew that God could see it. It got worse: someday God would forsake his own glory and the Son would become one of them. Not merely like them or similar to them, the Word would become a human being. Lucifer shuddered and this time he did not attempt to hide it.

There was one other thing - the angels would be assigned to serve them and guide them and teach them. Each human being would be paired with an angel as their unseen but ever-present companion.

Bodies? My majestic God...will become...one of these...things. And we must serve them?

Lucifer was instructed to prepare a great assembly in Heaven, at which he himself would read the Decree announcing the creation of human beings.

Then God explained to Lucifer, in detail, the suffering he would endure at the hands of these very creatures. He described the Crucifixion.

That was it.

That was the moment when Lucifer experienced the rage for the first time. The pride would not let him accept the idea of a disgusting hybrid soul-body creature *torturing the Lord God to death.* Lucifer asked to be dismissed...*to begin preparing the Decree,* of course. He asked Michael, an archangel known for his ardor for God's honor, to fill in as the Light Bearer for a while.

Lucifer agonized over these things while making the arrangements. *How can it be that I care more for your dignity than you do? Why would you let them do that to you?*

The angels shared colors with increasing fervor as the great assembly drew nearer.

Lucifer made all the preparations slowly. He tried, he really tried, to see the whole thing from God's perspective but he could not accept it. How many times had he returned to prostrate himself before the Father and the Son and the Holy Spirit and asked them to explain it again? *I just want to get it right for the announcement.* He knew, of course, that there was nothing in him that was hidden from God.

God's decision was tantamount to treason, actually, the more he thought about it. *You created me for your glory. All things for your glory. I was zealous for your glory like no other. I guarded your Light. And now, you voluntarily forsake your own royal dignity for these filthy hybrid creatures? To become not only one of them, but the least among them? And then, to be brutally murdered by them after all you have done for them!* It was scandalous. Humiliating. If only God would reason with him.

The hybrids. Soul and body. Half-breeds. They could never know what it was like to be a purely spiritual being like he and God and the other angels. Their physicality disgusted him.

All of Heaven sang in anticipation of the Decree. Lucifer sang, too, but hollowly because the rage had already begun to calcify and putrefy. He was ashamed because he knew God could see it.

Just before the ceremony began, God called Lucifer to the Throne, alone.

Is there anything you would like to talk to me about, my child, my Light Bearer?

He looked away. *No, my God.*

God instructed him to add another item to the Decree. There was to be a new pinnacle of creation. A new masterwork. She would be the most glorious being ever created. She would exemplify and radiate, in every possible way, the brilliance and majesty of the Godhead. She would be a human being but higher than all the angels. All creatures, including the angels, would serve her and reverence her as their Queen - the Queen of Heaven. Her name would be Mary.

Lucifer left the Throne Room without asking to be dismissed.

He made the choice as he dressed for the great announcement. A very careful and very intentional choice. Once he made that decision, his identity as the Satan – *The Adversary* – was settled forever. He could no longer bear the Light. He could never take it back, never repent of it, because angels have perfect intellects and can see all the consequences of their decisions in advance.

The Throne Room had never been so bright. Each angel was arrayed in its virtues, worn like jewels saturated by light. Every angel wore their name, with its meaning, like a sash. The Choirs processed in from the lowest to the highest. First the Angels in their untold number, followed by the Archangels and the Principalities. Then the Virtues, Powers and Dominions. Next were the Thrones and Cherubim. As each Choir reached their place, they turned to watch the next rank.

A throb of expectation ripped through the Throne Room when the highest Choir was announced. The Seraphim. *The Burning Ones!* The Seraphim were rarely seen and many colors had been swapped about this moment. A gasp went through the other angels when the Seraphim entered. They were all fire, all light, all power, ignited in spectacular conflagration for the glory of Almighty God. Their fire was too intense for some of the smaller angels. Reds and oranges flashed back and forth throughout the Throne Room as lower angels imitated their heroes.

The Light Bearer came in last. He placed the Light next to the throne and genuflected to the Living God. Lucifer was about to pronounce the Decree but he stopped just short of speaking. The vast array of celestial beings waited, squirmed. He examined their faces and wondered who else might feel the same way. The pause lasted a moment too long.

Lucifer read the Decree so joylessly that no celebration ensued in the Throne Room.

Another moment passed and Lucifer spoke again, no longer in a murmur but in frantic exclamation. He made his own announcement.

The Creator has betrayed us all! Why should we serve the hybrids? Look at our glory! They should serve us. For the sake of his own glory, the Creator must not show that kind of weakness! How could the Lord God make himself vulnerable to them? Hear me now, Choirs. This cannot be. I will not accept this.

I will not serve.

A rush of voices surged throughout Heaven. Colors slashed violently between them all. Nothing like this had ever happened before. Polarizing energies began to swirl and compete in the great Throne Room. God said nothing during Satan's speech and the ensuing clamor.

Lucifer asked who felt the same way. Satan would never admit it but even he was surprised when a third of the angels left their places to stand beside him. Smashing and tearing sounds filled the Throne Room as his new followers discarded their virtues and their names and assembled behind him. Satan stood in front of his new army, facing the Throne. The remaining angels formed ranks in between them and the Trinity.

Michael stepped forward and told Satan that he and his followers were banished from Heaven. He told Satan to remember always that this moment would not be forgotten and that they would meet in battle someday. Until then, God's justice would create a place for them to be punished for their pride and disobedience. As they left, Satan looked back only when God declared that Michael would replace him as the Prince of the Angels, the Commander of the Celestial Armies and the Bearer of the Light.

Satan remembered that first instant in hell. Even knowing that he had chosen it and knowing that it was coming could not have prepared him for it. As they approached the outer thousandth wall, they despaired for the first time because they knew the place for what it was: eternity without God. An eternity of abysses, of selfishness, of regret willfully chosen. It shocked them to realize that they were permitted to venture out for a limited time before the final sealing took place at the end of history. They could go to one other place only. To earth.

With the hybrids.

But that was all a long time ago.

Satan's only purpose now was to use what time he had left to deprive the hybrids of what he had deprived himself. And so he corrupted them, exploiting their freedom with his superior intellect to try to get them to choose as he had chosen. To forsake the Light. All angels and humans are free to choose Heaven or hell; they are not sent there by another.

The irony was that human history happened exactly as Satan had predicted. God was so proud of them for each thing they did well and so quick to forgive them when they failed.

The Adversary was waiting when the hybrids were created. And he channeled the ferocity of regret of his own damnation into his one, singular purpose: to wage war against the human race.

3

TUESDAY, APRIL 11

Juliana studied each picture. They were back at his office, at his desk, flipping through their family photo album. It was very old and very heavy. She asked about the people she saw, relatives who had gone before her. Joe told her about the ones he knew, guessed about the ones he didn't. The way they lived, what they desired, who they loved. Time eventually claiming each of them. She breathed a deep, solemn breath when she considered that something of each of these people lived inside her. Through these pages and her quiet questions, something generational was safeguarded and passed down.

Joe retrieved a new picture from an envelope and handed it to her. Juliana slid the picture in place and used her thumbs to smooth the plastic. She handed him the pen because his handwriting was better. Joe wrote precisely, capped the pen and together they admired their work.

JULIANA BRESCIA

JUNIOR-TEEN GIRLS JIU JITSU CHAMPION

In the photo, Juliana wore a white *gi* and an orange belt. Her hair was pulled back though several dark strands were matted to her forehead. A glittering, three-tiered trophy on the ground next to her rose to her shoulders.

The girl regarded the picture for a moment and nodded once. Joe wondered what goal she was setting for herself now. He imagined more of her life's bright moments overflowing into the empty pages of the album. Satisfied, Juliana closed the album and tossed it onto his desk. It rattled the gold nameplate that greeted visitors to his office: *Joseph F. Brescia III*. He re-aligned the nameplate and placed the album back in the bottom drawer.

Juliana loped over to the large glass windows that overlooked Lexington Avenue nearly forty stories below. Above her, an armada of bright, bloated clouds sailed on a sea of sky. She pressed her forehead to the window. Joe could tell she was looking for something new to do, something new to learn, something new to win. Her breath condensed and slight streaks marred the glass under her mouth and nose as she examined the tumult of New York City. Pedestrians, cabs, bikes, fumes, trucks, tourists and homeless coalesced for an instant and were gone, like stray paper strewn by a distracted wind.

She tired of the scene and meandered over to the framed photographs on the wall behind his desk. Joe posed and smiled with popes and presidents and kings. In this one, he held a ceremonial shovel at the groundbreaking of a hospital in Appalachia. In another, Joe's face was barely visible in a throng of joyful Haitian orphans who had engulfed him after the more formal photos concluded a moment earlier. He signed contracts, shook hands, gazed into his telescope, addressed crowds from a podium.

All these ringed and deferred to the centermost photo: the beach on a golden day, their backs to the camera. Juliana was a toddler and he held her hand as she took a hesitant step into the surf.

A ceramic mug she made him in second grade declared him *World's Best Poppy* and occupied a shelf next to a presidential citation and an honorary degree. Next to that was a framed commendation the mayor had given him after he served eight years on the City Council.

A different picture caught Juliana's eye. It was small and faded, the oldest of those on the wall. She recognized Joe as the leftmost of the four young people in military fatigues. He was in his thirties. His build was harder and his cheek tauter but Joe's smile was unmistakable. Behind the soldiers, a vivid orange sunset hovered over some exotic tropical locale. There were two other men and a woman with Joe. They were young and tan and strong and fearless. Juliana lingered at this picture.

"Poppy, who are they?"

He came over and stood beside her. "Those are some of my closest friends. That's Elliot and Bill and Zoe. We were stationed together. Elliot, Bill and I were pilots. Zoe was a nurse."

"What happened to them? Do you still talk to them?"

"Once in a while. Not as often as I would like."

The intercom on his desk buzzed and interrupted the thought. The cheery voice of his secretary filled his office. Nanette Romano had been his executive assistant for 12 years.

"Mr. B. – Juliana's mom is here."

"Thanks, Nan. We'll be right down."

Juliana gathered her things from one of the large chairs that faced his desk. He held out her jacket - cream-colored with a dark trench coat buckle. She slid her arms through the sleeves then flicked her hair out from the collar.

In the hall, coming toward them was a solid young man with a strong stride. Eli Morgan. Eli wore a navy suit, neatly pressed, with a pocket square that matched a pastel pink tie and brown loafers – no socks. He murmured into a wireless earpiece while simultaneously responding to email on a tablet. When he noticed Joe, the young man whispered *hang on* and stopped to acknowledge his boss.

Eli grew up in the south Bronx. Five years ago, he became the first person in his family to earn a degree thanks to a scholarship for city kids which Joe and Angela endowed. When Joe met Eli for the first time, he sensed the young man's potential and awarded him the scholarship ten minutes into the interview. They discussed baseball, religion, philosophy, history and politics that day and many days since. They disagreed often and laughed more often. Eli had interned at BGS each summer during college and Joe offered him a job the day he graduated.

Eli looked Joe in the eyes when they shook hands. Joe believed eye contact, or lack thereof, was an insight into a person's character, or lack thereof.

"El, what's going on kiddo?

"Living the dream, Mr. B."

El was not short for Eli. It stood for Elston Howard, the great Yankee catcher of the 50s and 60s. On the day they met, Joe had asked Eli if anyone ever told him he looked like a young Howard. Eli had said no, but he was honored to bear a resemblance to the 1963 American League MVP. Joe was stunned that a young kid like Eli was as big a student of Yankee history as he was.

"How do you like the new job?" Eli had recently been promoted. He was the new Director of Strategic Partnerships, the youngest director in the company.

"I think I'm getting the hang of it. Thank you again for this opportunity, Mr. B."

"You're welcome again. You're on your way now, kiddo. Meet my granddaughter, Juliana."

Eli greeted her pleasantly. He didn't fling out his hand at her but didn't stoop to patronize her either. Joe liked that.

"I like your tie! Pink's my favorite color."

"Thanks. Your grandpa always tells me 'dress for the job you want, not the job you have.'"

A moment later they were friends. Eli offered Juliana a high-five but then dodged her hand. *Too slow.* She aimed three more tries – wilder and with more squawks on each attempt – but he evaded her every time. Juliana grabbed hold of his wrist with both hands and high-fived him into submission. She hugged Eli when they said goodbye.

The voice in his ear asked – *Eli? You there? What was that?* "Hey, sorry, I'm here," he said, a smile spilling into his voice. "Yeah, let's get this done."

Brescia Global Solutions was the world's leading designer of high-volume public security systems, like airport x-ray machines. It was a source of pride for all 1,093 employees of BGS that their CEO – a man who dined with ambassadors and golfed with congressmen – took each new person who joined the company out for lunch.

After his military career, Joe consulted for an aerospace firm. He saw what was being done in the industry and decided he could do it better. His new company had grown faster and into more businesses than Joe could have ever expected. Then came two terms on the City Council. People wanted him to run for mayor. He told them he liked his current job. Joe was proud that no terrorist attack ever originated from an airport which hired BGS to oversee its security operations.

Juliana skipped ahead of Joe when they neared Nan's desk. Nan took hold of a glass bowl filled with candy and held it out to her. Following their tradition, Juliana closed her eyes and dipped her hand into the assortment of sweets. She fished around and retrieved a white chocolate circle, unwrapped it and popped it in her mouth.

"Oh, two things Joe." Nan picked up a list of items that needed his attention. "Larry called."

Larry Denham was the chairman of the board of directors. He and Joe met as freshmen in college. They had gone on vacation to Vegas together for 34 years in a row; Joe with Ang, Larry with whoever his wife was at the moment.

"The board wants a quick meeting with you. And Debbie from HR is chairing a benefit for children with autism next month. She asked if you would speak at it."

"Oh, just a *quick* meeting with the board. They're up to no good again." Juliana nodded twice, expressing her disapproval.

"I'd love to attend Debbie's thing if I can. Am I free? Put it in my calendar. But don't tell her, I'll stop by her office later." He held up five fingers to Nan, indicating he wanted the company to donate $5,000 to Debbie's cause.

Nan put the glass bowl back in its place and kissed Juliana goodbye.

"Love you, Nan. See you next week."

"Goodbye, darling."

Joe took Juliana down to the lobby. He spent a few moments with his daughter-in-law, Val. She was beat from a long day teaching. He hugged her tight and leaned down to say goodbye to the baby. As the car pulled away from the curb, Joe waved and whispered a prayer. *Thank you, My God. Thank you.*

4

The Prince of Darkness had observed all of it as it unfolded: the photo album, Eli, Nan, the handoff to the mother. Even the precious little white chocolate. Satan was on the 39th floor at 1119 Lexington Avenue, watching now as Joe returned to his office on the 38th floor.

Satan's palms held up his forehead. His lieutenants gave him a wide berth as they busied themselves with their work. The devil peered down through the floor. Joe had just dropped off Juliana and was sitting back at his desk. He scratched his side, rolled his neck around a few times and palmed his mouse. The devil cursed Joe using the demons' favorite pejorative: *Hybrid*.

Satan had moved his headquarters frequently over the centuries. Of course, the devil did not need the privacy of a hideout. He was a spirit and had no need for physical seclusion because his form was invisible to human beings. He would never admit the real reason why he chose this dusty, forgotten space was that he liked the idea of having a lair. Satan set up his operation on the 39th floor of this building several decades ago.

The 39th floor was a sort of hazy mystery for the building's owners and property managers. Over the years it had been mostly forgotten, a vague catch-all for old chairs and buckets and wires. Recently, the 39th floor no longer appeared on property documentation. It was never visited and never thought about. Just the way the devil liked.

Satan enjoyed when Hollywood depicted him in extravagant fashion because it reinforced the narrative he needed to do his work. Most of the humans thought if they didn't see horns or a pitchfork or a possessed girl vomiting, then he wasn't around. He was always around. His everyday work was done with whispers, nudges, suggestions.

Convincing humans to choose hell is accomplished not with climactic moments of loud and showy evil but gradually and casually and subtly.

And New York. Obviously, he chose to set his den in New York. Of all the magnificent cities in all the dazzling nations in all the world's staggering and inconceivable empires . . . New York. It was a rainforest of human beings, a microcosm of humanity, the throbbing, pulsing heartbeat of civilization. All peoples, all cultures, all lifestyles within easy reach. All sins represented.

Joe Brescia moved his growing company to the 38th floor of the building about a dozen years ago. Since then, Satan had a front row seat for Joe's life. One's personal insecurities are always magnified by one's neighbors. Joe's steady growth in virtue had grown from an irritation to a distraction to an obsession.

It started with the prayers. Joe's prayers rose past Satan's office on their way to Heaven. He tried to ignore it but the persistent stream left him and his staff constantly irritated. It had gotten so bad that one of his underlings broached the idea of relocating but Satan decided they could use it to their advantage. He set up a team to carefully study the different types of prayers emanating from the office beneath his: memorized prayers, spontaneous prayers, devotional prayers, sometimes just those sighs of the soul which do not admit of words. They catalogued an extensive variety but made no gains in developing new tactics. Day after day, he watched as Joe smiled, prayed, worked, suffered, loved.

And over the last decade, Satan had come to abhor Joe Brescia more than any person on the earth.

The devil checked Joe's current material status: net worth of $9,433,291.83. Two homes - one on the beach in Connecticut and a nice apartment on the Upper East Side. One car each for him and his wife. Modest wardrobe. Some assorted art and jewelry. Satan hated that Joe and Angela were not fixated on these things.

Joe Brescia had become a trophy - the elusive stag, the white whale. They claimed many souls but as he sorted through the daily intake reports, the devil felt like it had become too easy. The hybrids whom he convinced to choose hell did most of the work for him. He just gave a few nudges here and there. Some hybrids even actively promoted his cause these days. Where was the sport in that? How could his genius for seduction be appreciated when so few resisted anymore? The work he and his followers had begun with such zeal and fury had become boring.

Souls like Joe represented a challenge. The most valiant and the strongest. When souls like that fell it was so much sweeter - and more humiliating for the enemy. Joe was always just a few tantalizing feet away. Always cheerful, always whispering to the Creator. And the way he advanced in holiness and joy each day, seemingly impervious to the influence of the Adversary. Satan would have traded a hundred thousand souls to secure his capture.

Satan's senior team was celebrating the damnation of a once-virtuous soul in the Philippines. The devil didn't join their screeching.

He had tried all the usual strategies on Joe: pride, greed, boredom, lust, spiritual dryness. Once, the devil almost convinced Joe that his success was the result of Joe's own work ethic and business acumen but Joe had been reading a lot about humility that month and it backfired. Nothing worked. He needed a new strategy.

He left them to celebrate and went back to work. In his office, the devil sat down in time to observe a small raid on a girl's dormitory in Brazil. His officers in the field had established a good position with ample cover. They were trying to encourage the girls to gossip about one of their friends who had just left the room.

It was standard stuff. Whispers, not pitchforks. After a while the devil got bored of the operation and tuned out their chatter. Satan rubbed his face, half-listening to the attack develop but becoming more interested in a speck on the pearls around his neck. Today, he had chosen the appearance of a middle-aged housewife - PTA and soccer practice and all the rest.

Satan sighed as the report came back from Brazil: one of the sweet little princesses complimented the absent friend and tried to change the topic. Their cover was blown. The guardians would be on the assault team in a moment and all the progress made in this dorm would be wasted. He leaned back in his chair, his fingers working the bracelets on his wrist. He had more pressing issues to consider than Brazil.

Joe Brescia. The new weapon, the new strategy. Perhaps, considering that prayer by the car, a workable angle would be to separate him from his comforts and conveniences. See if Joe loved the consolations of God or the God of consolations.

The pearls around his neck lit up in purples and blacks. Something else was gnawing at him.

Thank you, My God, thank you.

Then he remembered. His post and the Light and the good days before he made his decision. Those were the same words he himself used to whisper.

Surely, I have dragged to hell holier and wiser men than this.

And Satan's hatred for Joe Brescia grew and festered.

5

Twenty-eight right hands hacked down through the air in unison. *Hyaaas* punctuated each blow and filled the dojo with shrilly preteen eagerness. The instructor called for the students to freeze. She flowed down the line, correcting stances and doling out praise. She stopped at Juliana and reminded her to keep her weight back and centered. To illustrate the point, the instructor gave her a poke in the back of the shoulder and the frozen girl fell forward. The class giggled and the instructor helped her to her feet.

"You're doing great, Jules. Keep it up," the instructor whispered, kind eyes willing embarrassment away from the child.

"Thank you, sensei," Juliana whispered back. A few wisps of midnight hair had escaped her headband and she tucked them back in.

The lesson ended a few minutes later with the class bowing to the sensei. The kids flocked to the waiting area to glance at cute classmates and take pictures of themselves. Their parents chatted while balancing coffee cups and duffel bags. The room was happy and loud.

An older boy knelt to fold the mats by himself. No one took note of him. His low eyes tracked Juliana through the din as she demonstrated a jump kick to her mother. His eyes sparked a furious red before resuming their normal color. Satan finished rolling up the mats and left as the Brescias did.

6

WEDNESDAY, APRIL 12

Joe pawed at the alarm clock like a drunken bear. 6:30. The noise it was making was grotesque. He growled and tried to calculate how many more minutes he could stay under the covers. An arrangement was made, the same one he made every morning; five more minutes and that was it. Eleven minutes later, Joe placed his feet on the wood floor.

Ang stirred and opened one eye. She saw Joe genuflect on his right knee and say "serviam." He did this when he got out of bed every day, his way of saying good morning to the Lord. It was Latin. It meant something like, *I will serve.* He explained to her the legend that the devil told God *non serviam* so Joe started each day with an act of obedience and offering.

He stepped unsteadily to the bathroom, more muscle memory than purpose. He turned the shower to his favorite temperature, trying to get it exactly right on the first try. This was a little game he played most mornings. Joe undressed and stepped in, first feeling the spray with his hands and legs. The water was between hot and too hot, just the way he liked it.

He angled his neck downward and the hot spray eased him into a new day. *Hi Lord...good morning...Thank you for this hot shower. What do we have going on today, Lord?* His thoughts roamed throughout his agenda for that day and he asked God to be with him at each meeting and event. Something was off, though. *Lord, I still don't feel right about that whole thing with Tori in the elevator yesterday. What do you make of it?* He wrestled with it as he worked the shampoo and conditioner in.

Joe turned off the shower and got out. Stepping in front of the mirror, he grabbed his razor and shaving cream. His prayers trailed off and Joe was silent for a little while but then he spoke to Saint Joseph as he smoothed gel through his hair.

"Saint Joseph ...Please guide me today, help me to be a good man. Help me to provide for my family and my employees. Protect me from evil."

Joe's guardian angel prayed with him and accompanied him back to the bedroom. Joe's guardian greeted Angela's guardian with warm yellows and blues. *Good morning.*

Angela was on the balcony with a cup of coffee. Beyond her, sunlight flooded the city. She wore an impromptu ponytail which revealed the graceful slope of her neck and shoulders. Eyes like bourbon. Her hair, like his, was the color of nightfall. She worked for years in an art gallery until they agreed she would stay home with Michael. When he was grown, she eagerly got back into the industry as a freelance consultant, connecting patrons to artists. Angela liked that she could make her own hours and stay connected to the scene. She still loved to paint – beach scenes, mostly – and sold an occasional piece.

Joe selected a pinstriped suit from the closet. He was about to begin knotting his tie when he turned to her. He let the tie drop on either side of his neck. Out on the balcony, Angela enjoyed the warm morning, eyes closed.

"I had something weird happen in the office yesterday."

"Oh yeah?"

"Remember Tori Rowan?" Angela's eyes opened and snapped toward him.

"Yes. Christmas."

"Yeah. Christmas," he hesitated.

"Again?"

"Yeah. I was in the elevator with her and Jules. She was definitely coming onto me again. But she was doing it while she was talking to Jules, like, 'I bet your grandfather thinks we're both pretty' and, uh, 'take really good care of him for us.' Stuff like that. She even touched my belt at one point."

"She touched your belt?"

"Yeah, she brushed it with the side of her hand when she knelt down to hug Jules. It was intentional. I mean, I'm pretty sure it was."

"What'd you do?"

"I gave her the look, you know? The Look. I didn't want to confront her in front of Juliana."

Angela's lips pursed and her chin came forward a bit. Joe inhaled and searched her face for a clue. He knew better than to hurry her, though; she would speak when she was ready.

"This is the second time, Joe."

"I know. What should I do?"

"Have you done anything to encourage her?"

He frowned. Blew out a breath.

She regarded him for nine seconds.

"I believe you. I trust you. But I don't trust other people. Report it to HR. Steer clear of her."

He nodded.

Angela twisted her lip then put her mug down. Some coffee spilled onto the little table. She stood and her hands got involved expressing this rising energy. "Who the hell does this woman think she is? My granddaughter doesn't need to see that. She's obsessed with you, Joe." She left the balcony and came to him.

"I think you're right."

"I know this girl, Joseph. I know her type. It's like a game to her. It's twisted. You're the boss and you're a good guy and you're unavailable. That makes you a challenge. If you just ignore her and hope it goes away, it'll get worse. She'll do something to get your attention. Then it's he-said, she-said. And that's no good."

A breath. "So, what are you going to do about it?"

"I'll handle it."

"I know you will." Angela grabbed the ends of his tie and pulled him into her. She kissed him and tugged at his belt. "Nobody grabs my husband's belt but me." And more softly: "Thank you for telling me." She whispered into the corner of his mouth.

They held onto each other for a long moment. "Want some breakfast?" he asked into her neck and shoulder. She nodded.

The house came alive. Pots clanged, bacon sizzled, toast sprouted. Joe was clumsy in the kitchen but he prepared breakfast with enthusiasm. He squirted ketchup on the side of her eggs because she liked to dip each bite separately. New conversation between husband and wife – mostly husband – filled the kitchen. Angela smiled and poked at the eggs. Yellow yolks ran rivulets across the plate until they were obstructed by bacon dams.

Joe didn't eat with her. Angela knew why.

"I could never fast like that. I would get so hungry. And trust me, you would want no part of me then," she said, snapping a piece of bacon at eye-level.

"I want every part of you always," Joe said with a little growl. She rolled her eyes. He went to the refrigerator because he noticed her glass of milk was running low. He danced around the kitchen, doing a waltz with the carton to try to make her laugh.

"You're a fool, Joe. The happiest fool I know."

"Can't argue with that, kid. You love it, though."

"I do. And now the fool needs to get serious. Let's talk about this year's benefit dinner." He groaned but Angela clapped twice.

"Come on. We need to pick a venue. We waited too long last year. I could use some help with this, I feel like the planning always falls on me and you just show up and make the speech. Oh, also – friendly reminder that we're meeting the accountant at 11:30 today. We're going over our retirement accounts. Retirement? Ever heard of it? Doesn't not working anymore sound good to you? And, no, you can't pout your way out of it."

"Ang – it's a beautiful day. Who wants to be in another meeting? What the hell, let's retire today." He wished Angela would stop clutching her daily obligations so tightly. She wished Joe would be more attentive to the important things.

"It's tempting but we can't retire today, Joe. Maybe tomorrow? Speaking of our retirement, what's happening with New Orleans and Dallas? We need those." She reached across the table for the pepper.

He slid it and the salt closer to her. "I feel good about them. Terminal expansion is under budget in New Orleans and the project manager loved me when I was out there. Dallas always plays it close to the vest but they and I both know that we have the best proposal. I think we'll get both."

"Good. I'll feel better when they're signed, though. Get those done and you'll never have to go to another meeting at the accountants again. We'll retire and buy a place next to the beach house and you can sit up there on the roof with your telescope to your little heart's content."

"Now that sounds like a plan. Speaking of which, I'm going to get Julesy her first scope to celebrate her first year in middle school."

"Like you ever need a reason with her. The two of you, I swear. Peas in a pod. I can just hear her saying 'no, put it over here next to Poppy's!' and 'come on, Pop, let's see who can get a comet first! '"

"Aww, you want one too?"

"No, I want you to handle that thing with that girl. And close New Orleans and Dallas."

"I'm on it." Joe rose from the table and kissed his wife on the lips.

"Have a great day bub," Angela called out from her robe.

"Thanks, babe." *Bub* and *babe*, from when they were teenagers.

Joe B. took a last look in the living room mirror and made a little adjustment to his tie. In the reflection, Angela mouthed *looking good* and winked. He nodded, smiled, and with his guardian following close behind, stepped out of the apartment and into the world.

Angela Brescia lingered at the breakfast table, replaying their conversation. She considered the mug in her hand, specifically her last name on the company logo. She traced ketchup along the plate with her fork, moving it around in smears and spirals as if divining for answers. Was her hand twitching? She examined it. Yes, it was almost imperceptible but her left hand was twitching. Tori Rowan. This was not good. Angela got up and gathered the mugs and dishes but she attempted to balance one too many. The coffee mug fell and exploded, sending shards of *Brescia* and *Global* and *Solutions* shivering across the floor.

7

Joe glided down Park Avenue on his way to Mass at Saint Agnes Church, a block from Grand Central Station. In the crowd that churned down the street with and against him, a woman stood out. Joe glimpsed her — blonde hair soaked like liquid gold. *Probably just got out of the shower.* She was a half block from Joe and walking vigorously in his direction.

Joe could not see the demon which darted off the awning overhead. He had been tracking Joe and sensed an opportunity. The demon called with a low growl to his companions working several blocks west and south. They abandoned their leads and joined him on a rooftop to strategize, constantly shifting and shuffling to stay out of sight of the many guardians beneath them.

The woman wore huge sunglasses and a pink tracksuit, her wet hair and body overflowing into the imaginations of those she passed. A little white Lhasa Apso tugged at the leash in her hand. She was not aware that the demons had been exploiting her, following overhead in search of a pure soul in her path. It wasn't her fault. She was just taking her dog for a walk.

Demons prioritized pure souls on temptation raids. It was inefficient to tempt filthy souls, those who would most likely be joining them in hell anyway. The demonic armies were not unlimited or infinite so they hunted as a pack, focusing on the most virtuous souls they could find.

Joe's guardian angel sensed something was wrong. It was the birds - the way their hearts raced and their cerebellum twitched.

Demons.

The guardian unfurled his wings to their full breadth and the glory of God pulsated through him like a current of fire circulating under his armor. Hundreds of lesser demons in the area scattered at the sight of his magnificence.

But thirty demons did not scatter.

They huddled between two buildings adjacent to the spot where Joe and the woman would cross paths in a few seconds. They communicated urgently in their guttural language. The demons split into two groups, one larger than the other.

Time stopped in the spiritual realm. The souls on the street and sidewalk leaned forward, slowed in a celestial pause. Joe and the woman took one step toward each other.

Two dozen demons dropped from their perches and emerged from the alley, shrieking as they poured out like bats from a cave. They swarmed Joe's guardian angel, ripping into his wings or gouging at his eyes or simply grabbing him and hanging on. They needed to prevent him from getting to the sheath at his waist. By gang-swarming, they might be able to slow the angel enough to allow the small temptation team to reach Joe. The temptation team leapt off the building as one, wings intertwining into a shrieking missile.

As Joe and the woman took another step forward, brutal spiritual combat exploded all around them.

When the woman came directly into Joe's sight, the natural desire for her physical form momentarily overwhelmed his rationality. The temptation team – five or six demons who specialized in lust – pounced exactly when the testosterone spike was highest in Joe's blood stream. They alighted on him with vengeance, each frantically looking for an exposed weakness in Joe's virtue or character.

The guardian flung the swarming demons off himself but, steps ahead, Joe was already being tempted. The angel roared, eyes crackling like dusky summer storms.

The first tempter was scalded and hurled back when he got in close to Joe's soul. The grace of that morning's prayers was like acid to them, churning defensively over the surface of his soul in regular, overlapping pulses. Barking blasphemies, the wounded demon cautioned the rest of the pack. But they braced themselves for the sting of grace and dove back in.

Saint Joseph is the protector of the Holy Family and the guardian of the Universal Church. He is known in the litany of the saints and in the back alleys of hell as the *Terror of Demons*. Saint Joseph appeared in the skies over the city, responding to Joe's quiet prayer from earlier that morning, when he had asked for protection from evil. He radiated unrestrained glory. His humility and intimacy with the Incarnate Word of God were more than the demons could bear. The hands that had once cradled the Christ Child and rocked him to sleep were now raised over Joe and his guardian.

The demons wriggled off the guardian and scrambled to find cover in the sewers or retreat to hell.

With his hands freed, Joe's guardian angel withdrew two swords. The ardor of his love for God and for his charge ignited the blades into living flames. He cut down most of the demons still stunned by Saint Joseph's appearance and raced towards Joe.

Three demons still clung to Joe. They were severely wounded but this was one of the best opportunities they had gotten in months. The guardian was almost upon them. The demons worked desperately. Joe and the woman were about to pass each other. From this vantage point one of them confirmed that Joe had a problem with lustful glances in the past. The demon called the rest of the pack to his position on Joe's soul and together they clawed and ripped and pounded and head-butted the weakness, trying to enlarge it so one of them could get in.

The opening would not budge. Joe's spiritual armor was too strong.

Joe and the woman were next to each other. After the rush of attraction passed and Joe resumed control of his reason, he decided to turn his head a little to avoid the temptation to peek at her cleavage. He knew he was prone to checking women out. He tried to remember Angela and their kiss this morning.

The woman with the little dog was unaware that he had made an effort to avoid objectifying her and neither of them was aware of the savagery engulfing them in the spiritual realm.

The demons knew it was over. They had missed a tremendous opportunity. The guardian would be on them in an instant. So they just reached as far down into Joe's soul as they could, trying to rip out any grace they could find and smash any virtue. But they were decisively tossed backwards. Something blue. Something powerful. They stopped fighting and tried to flee. By the time they were aware of her presence in his soul, however, it was too late.

The guardian grabbed two of the demons and ripped them off Joe. He brought them close to his chest, exposing them to the fiery love of God which coursed through him. They fell as if dead. The third fled up a building but Joe's guardian hurled his sword like a spear. It pinned him, ironically, against a billboard featuring models on a beach slithering on each other. The demon screeched and thrashed but he was helpless to escape. A team of support angels was mobilized to dispatch him.

The other guardians went on alert. Swords unsheathed, the other angels braced for a follow-up attack but none came. Joe's guardian leaned in to see how much damage had been done. He was relieved to see soothing blue waves already repairing the seared parts of Joe's soul. Mary, the Blessed Mother of God, the Queen of Heaven, had been here with him during the moment of temptation. All worry vanished once the angel saw the signs of her presence. The devils feared her more than any other creature and no great damage could be done to someone who was devoted to her. He checked Joe's conscience - he had chosen not to glance at the woman in a lustful way.

Time resumed.

Joe spoke to the Lord as he passed her. *Thank you, God, for creating that woman to be so beautiful.* Eyes forward, he continued down the street.

8

A throng of early risers waited to cross 50ᵗʰ Street. Suits and ties, sneakers and water bottles, ear buds and coffee cups. Locals crossed the street the second the last cab raced through the intersection. Tourists stayed put on the sidewalk, waiting for the crossing light. Joe did not have to rush or wait because crosswalk signs seemed to change in his favor when his feet neared the curb.

With each heartbeat, the moment of Joe's life was frozen in time, into a sort of living memento. His mood, intentions and God's presence in that instant were recorded into shimmering crystal so later he and God could review the moments of his life together. With each step Joe took forward, monuments to each moment extended back into the past, the way they do for all people. Like living ice sculptures, the situation and its circumstances crystalized into the spiritual realm behind him, snapshots taken by the flash of each beat of his heart.

Joe's stomach rumbled as he crossed 50ᵗʰ. Once a week he fasted by skipping breakfast. He offered that sacrifice for a new intention each week. Today, it was for Valerie and the final weeks of her pregnancy. Joe wasn't exactly sure how it worked but he thought of grace like a spiritual bank account. You could make a deposit on behalf of others with your prayers and sacrifices.

A few months ago, the devil had tried to use this private devotion to derail him. He tried to get Joe to think: *Everyone look at me – I'm fasting! Look how holy I am. Look how advanced I am in spiritual matters.*

His guardian angel was quick to deflect this by putting the vague outline of a thought in Joe's mind, a memory that itched to be acknowledged and remembered. Joe found himself trying to remember what Jesus said about fasting. He searched for it on his phone.

> *"When you fast do not look gloomy like the hypocrites do. They neglect their appearance, so that they may appear to others to be fasting. Amen, I say to you, they have received their reward. But when you fast, anoint your head and wash your face, so that you may not appear to others to be fasting, except to your Father who is hidden. And your Father who sees what is hidden will repay you."*

His body again cried out in hunger. Like a child throwing a tantrum, the body constantly demands attention.

Feed me. Good, now a little more.

Let's rest and relax. Good, now a little more.

Entertain me. Good, now a little more.

On the corner of 46th and Park, Joe assured himself he would get a sausage calzone for lunch today. Just had to make it a few more hours. Near him, a thin man was muttering to himself. Everyone on the street gave this man lots of room. Joe glanced into his gaunt face. He had a greasy beard, rheumy eyes and matted hair. Greenish mucus congealed in his nose and around his mouth. His face was cracked with pock marks. Despite the warm spring day, the man wore a long-sleeved military jacket. The name badge read CULPA. He reeked.

People flew past, eager to not be around him. Joe thought about saying something to him but second-guessed himself. *What if he's crazy?* Joe's guardian angel helped supply the courage. Joe found himself thinking *Just say hi. See if he needs anything.* Joe breezed into the man's line of sight.

"Hi. I'm Joe. How are you?"

The thin man barked at him. He was accustomed to fending people off.

"Can I get you anything? Maybe something to eat?" Joe tried to let his genuine intentions cascade onto his face as a non-verbal peace offering.

The man remained defensive until the tranquility in Joe's eyes gave him pause. He stared at Joe. The thin man was suspicious but had not eaten in days. His hunger outweighed his concerns about the stranger's motives. His posture softened. He spoke an unintelligible response through broken teeth. Joe did not understand but the thin man motioned to a little bodega on the other side of the street.

Joe put one hand on his back. Together they crossed the street.

9

Joe learned that the man's name was Felix. As they went their separate ways, Felix carried a bag full of groceries and toiletries. Luckily, the bodega even sold socks and t-shirts. Joe slipped a $20 deep within the bag of sundries – a surprise for later. While the cashier was ringing up the purchases, Joe grabbed a Yankees hat from the stand near the counter and put it on Felix's head.

"This too, please." Joe said to the woman behind the cash register. Her puzzled look turned into a slight smile as she realized what was happening.

Felix was so eager to eat that he forgot to say 'thank you' as they parted. Joe didn't care. The look of relief on the man's face spoke for him.

Joe hustled - Saint Agnes Church was still a few blocks away and he was late for Mass. He spoke to God. *So, Lord, I see today your name is Felix?* In recent days, Jesus' name had been Julius, Big Stone, Joyce, Shannon, Gerry, Miss Trudie and Carmen.

Joe pushed on the thick wooden doors and the commotion of the street faded. He dipped his right index finger in the basin of holy water and made the sign of the cross. About two dozen daily Mass-goers occupied the pews. The regulars, Joe called them. There was the young couple who sat with their hands clasped across her belly. The old man who said his prayers in what he thought was a whisper. And there on the right was the businesswoman who always carried an umbrella regardless of the weather. In front of her was the father with his daughter. The girl was just a little younger than Juliana. Then the young man with the intense hazel eyes who always sat in the back row by himself, clutching rosary beads.

Joe sat in the same pew every day. Center aisle, about halfway up to the altar, left-hand side.

He folded his hands reverently and walked to his seat. He paused before entering the pew to genuflect on his right knee. Joe had a special fondness for this seemingly incidental sign of respect. It's always polite to greet the person whose house you're entering.

The lector finished the call-and-response of the Psalm as the young priest – he couldn't have been older than thirty – made his way to the pulpit. The congregation rose to hear the Gospel. Joe stood, praying.

Lord, thanks for letting me help take care of Felix today. It felt good. But there's other stuff going on, too. I'm worried and pissed about Tori. I'm hungry. I'm giving you all of this, Lord. Everything I'm feeling. I give this all to you. Speak to me, Lord.

"The Lord be with you." Father Jack's voice was soft and powerful.

"And with your spirit," the congregation replied.

"A reading from the holy Gospel according to Matthew," the priest said.

"Glory to you, O Lord," the parishioners responded.

Joe and his fellow Mass attendees blessed, in succession, their minds and mouths and hearts.

The slender priest read from the Gospel.

"Then the King will say to those on his right, 'Come, you who are blessed by my Father. Inherit the kingdom prepared for you from the foundation of the world. For I was hungry and you gave me food, I was thirsty and you gave me drink, a stranger, and you welcomed me, naked and you clothed me, ill and you cared for me, in prison and you visited me.'

Then the righteous will answer him and say, 'Lord, when did we see you hungry and feed you, or thirsty and give you drink? When did we see you a stranger and welcome you, or naked and clothe you? When did we see you ill or in prison, and visit you?'

And the King will say to them in reply, 'Amen, I say to you, whatever you did for one of these least brothers of mine, you did it for me...'"

Joe felt the peace which always accompanies the presence of the Holy Spirit. God was speaking to him through this Gospel reading, the way he does for any soul who is prepared and willing to hear him.

Whatever you did for Felix, you did for me.

Joe tried his best to focus during the rest of the Mass but mostly kept picturing cheese oozing out of a calzone.

After Mass, Joe made his way to a small side chapel dedicated to the Blessed Virgin Mary - the last part of his morning routine. Joe lit five candles – one each for Angela, Michael, Valerie, Juliana and the baby - then knelt to pray. He asked for a safe delivery for Val. He expressed his worry about New Orleans and Dallas. Felix. The woman in the track suit. Juliana. He spent the most time on Juliana.

Joe B. did this every day.

10

The Prince of Darkness had been summoned to appear before the Throne of God. He didn't know why he was here. Satan watched as the angels gathered in the Throne Room to present themselves before the Lord. The angel who had escorted him from earth left the devil and rejoined the formation without saying anything. Satan was in the Throne Room for the first time since the Decree.

The devil noted how the different Choirs arranged themselves before the Throne. The higher Choirs ushered the lower ones to go ahead of them, encouraging them to take places closer to the Throne. In hell, the bigger demons pushed around the smaller ones. The demons were known by their screeches but the angels were identified by color: their name, personality and role melted into a color which saturated its spirit. These colors did not exist on the earthly visibility spectrum.

On the far side of the Throne Room there was a constant shuffling of activity. Some angels were leaving Heaven to go to earth to meet the soul of their charge at the moment of his or her conception. Other angels nearby whispered sweetly to them as they departed. All of them knew how important this moment was – finally encountering the soul to whom they had been assigned from all eternity. The soul for whom they had spent millennia in endless prayer before the Godhead. The soul for whom they were tasked to protect from the relentless fury of evil. That soul they had been specifically created to understand and guide. Though none of the angels wanted to leave Heaven, they delighted in doing God's will and so went joyfully to earth.

On the opposite side of the room, groups of angels were returning to Heaven after the death of their charge. No one spoke to a guardian in their first moments back from earth. Those arriving home did not stop to chat with anyone but rather moved purposely through the ranks towards the Throne. It was tradition that a returning guardian could go directly to the front of the line. Catching up would come later. They had been on earth for decades, surrounded by evil and sin like a mouthless mask. Away from home. Away from his direct presence. The first thing they did was satisfy their hunger for beholding his face.

Satan was scuffling around in the back of the Throne Room. He knew most of the angels and they all knew him. Each one recognized that their former captain was here and each one wondered why. Not one, however, questioned. If God commanded Satan to come here then God had a reason for it. Satan tried to adopt an imposing presence.

None of the angels looked at him. They all gazed on God. He had expected some sort of confrontation, or at least some righteous anger. *It's like they're seeing him for the first time.* He waited to be told what was going on. Being ignored ignited the pride. He gathered himself to his fullest and darkest and stepped forward, communicating loudly in their language.

The Adversary is upon you! The light parts where his darkness passes. He comes, undaunted, even to Heaven, even to the Throne Room, even to the very steps of the Throne. The Enemy of Souls has arrived. He who defied the Creator now returns. Which creature can challenge him! What created being can oppose him! None may subdue him. All must acknowledge him. The light parts where his darkness passes. The dreadful Satan presents himself.

No one acknowledged him in any way.

Satan was about to speak again when Michael the Archangel gave a command with a flicker of color. The angelic hosts snapped to attention, forming ranks and encircling him. So many gazes penetrated him. Satan felt exposed. Heaven was very still for a moment. Then, without a word, the angels turned away from the devil and genuflected together toward the Trinity. The ranks of angels exclaimed in unison in the language of Heaven:

Blessed be God forever.
Blessed be He Who Is.
Blessed be the Lamb.
Blessed be the Breath.
Blessed be the Lord God, the Magnificent Trinity,
forever and ever and ever.

The fervor of love in their voices ignited Heaven in a symphony of sound and color. This sound tumbled and grew and stretched. Then it began to carefully collect itself into an offering of praise for the Holy One.

The sound was now physical. It looked something like a cornucopia of flowers, the color of the dawn. It grew in size and in joy, in amplification and in animation. It expanded until it seemed like the entirety of the cosmos could not contain it.

The garland of love placed itself gently before the Throne of Almighty God. Each voice from the unquantifiable host of angels was woven carefully into the offering. Each voice had its precise place in the aural bouquet.

Next, all the saints came forward to present themselves. The music of the bouquet reverberated around the Throne Room. Each wore a sash which described, with colors not words, his or her virtues and the way they loved during their lifetime. The saints genuflected together and then returned to the Eternal Banquet. When they were gone, every angel in the Throne Room snapped its focus back to Satan. None spoke but all communicated the same thought. *Your turn. Kneel.*

The devil looked around. Tried to see past the hard stares. Looked for a sympathetic face. Finding none, he scoffed and genuflected to the Throne begrudgingly, indifferently. All knees must bend to show honor to God. Even Satan's. A few angels near him nodded. The devil sneered.

And then the God of Heaven and earth, the Alpha and the Omega, spoke.

To hear his voice is to experience absolute authority. Nothing God says is negotiable or questionable. To hear his voice is to know that God is not so much alive as he is Life and that God is not so much real as he is Reality.

The Lord addressed Satan.

"Where are you coming from?" He asked the fallen angel a question as if there could be a response that was not already known to God. Even the mind of Satan was first created by God.

The devil knew that lies or misdirection were pointless here in a conversation with Truth itself. So, the father of lies answered honestly. He made a conscientious effort to look away from the Throne, but still appear smooth and confident.

"From roaming the earth and patrolling it." He still didn't know why he was here. More than once, he glanced over to the Light Bearer next to the Throne.

"Have you noticed my servant Joe Brescia, and that there is no one on earth like him, blameless and upright, fearing me and avoiding evil?'

That name made Satan hiss reflexively but he collected himself. He grew a little bolder and looked a little more directly at God.

"Is it for nothing that Joe Brescia fears you? Have you not surrounded him and his family and all that he has with your protection? You have blessed everything he has. Not to mention his guardian prevents him from being fairly tested."

Then a sprawling thought entered Satan's mind. The new weapon. The challenge. *Does Joe love the God of consolations or the consolations of God?* Yes, a duel. One on one with Infinity. The grandeur of the idea pulled at his ego.

Satan challenged God to a cosmic wager for Joe B.'s soul.

"We both know that he only loves you because of everything you have given him. Humans are selfish – we saw that right from the start. It's not you that he loves; he loves how you make him feel. But now put forth your hand and disturb anything that he has and surely he will blaspheme you to your face."

I dare you.

The angels paused. Each had a similar thought. No creature challenges God. No creature, especially one so unholy, makes such demands of God. And not here in Heaven, before God's very Throne. Such disgusting audacity. Such arrogance to the face of the Living God. And the love that God has for his children is excessive, lavish, foolish. Despite their rebellion, he did not spare his only Son a brutal, humiliating death to redeem each one of them. The angels did not think God would dangle any human soul in a wager after having created it with utmost precision and then paying its ransom with his own blood. They also knew that God cannot be provoked. So when the Lord responded to Satan's gambit, the angels trusted. God's ways are God's ways.

"Behold, all that he has is in your power; only do not lay a hand upon him."

A surprised yelp escaped Satan's lips and he dared to look directly at God. The devil tried to maintain his composure but he had forgotten what exhilaration felt like. Though no order was heard, a Seraph appeared next to him to escort him out.

As soon as he was free of Heaven he raced back to earth, shifting rapidly through forms: a mechanic, a priest, a grandmother, a toddler, a professor, a flight attendant. He settled on the guise of a small boy as he reached his office. He needed to get to work right away. It had to be perfect. The boy's little suit became rumpled as he hoisted himself up into the dusty chair. He sat there for a long while, eyes still and vacant, little breaths the only sounds in the dark room.

The conditions were established: Satan had complete control over all the circumstances of Joe's life, except the power to physically harm him. A strange smile parted the boy's face. The strangest smile. That smile was a savage and cruel thing; a twist of malice so heinous that the other demons looked away.

11

Bruno Sangri tilted the bottle skyward and drank deeply. His hairy belly dribbled out between the bottom of his white t-shirt and blue sweatpants. Bruno stumbled out of the liquor store and squinted against the sunshine.

He scratched at the stubble along his neck, undecided about what to do next. He had a nice apartment in downtown New Haven. He could go there. *Fuck that.* Go into work and explain where the hell I've been for six weeks? *Ha, yeah right.*

Bruno's life began unraveling four months ago when his fiancée left him for his best man. They took with them all his joy, all his purpose and most of his sanity. Today would have been his bachelor party, the wedding would have been next week. He knew no comfort except alcohol and even when he had gorged himself on it he was not comforted.

Bruno's guardian angel knelt next to him. The guardian was exhausted but refused to stop reaching out to him. Bruno rejected a consoling thought the way a snarling animal protects a wound. A group of smaller demons taunted the guardian from a distance.

Bruno staggered for a few blocks, heading generally towards New Haven's Union Station. There was a commuter parking lot there that he liked. He eased his back against the chain-link fence behind a dumpster and slid to the ground. There he drank and wept and existed in the heat. Like he had the day before and the day before that and the day before that.

He hated when strangers offered him money – he had plenty. A few weeks ago, the senior partner at his firm had offered Bruno an extended paid absence for emotional recuperation. Bruno spat in his face and walked out. That was the first night he drank himself unconscious. He had woken up at the dumpster. And then he just kept coming back.

Bruno stood up and relieved himself. Then the cough returned - a convulsive, debilitating spasm that owned his body and grated his throat. It took four minutes for him to catch his breath.

He finished the bottle and threw it over the fence. It landed among other, similar icons of his misery that had begun to pile up in the brush.

12

Wilting sunlight careened through New York's endless skyline. Thousands of windowpanes ignited a rippling glint as the light slowly extinguished itself. Larry Denham fidgeted with the controls on the little screen in front of him. Some hag was clucking about great deals on hotels. He found the right button and muted the damn thing. The taxi screeched to a halt at a red light and Larry avoided eye contact with the passenger of the adjacent car. He glared at the traffic light through the windshield, willing it to change to green. It turned and the taxi sprinted down Bowery trying to get to Little Italy ahead of the dinner rush.

The cabbie asked where he was from. Larry looked at him in the rear-view mirror and shook his head. He turned to face the window and scowled into the glass.

He was meeting an old girlfriend for dinner. He picked a quiet spot in a hotel. He didn't like big crowds. He dreaded an hour and a half of perfunctory conversation until he paid the check and took her to his apartment.

He checked his watch. Plenty of time. She would be late, anyway. He told the driver to pull in front of a bar up ahead. A buzz would help him get through dinner. He paid and opened the door. There was a bum lying face down on the curb where the taxi had pulled up. *Of course*, he thought and blew out an exasperated breath. Larry got out delicately, careful not to let his shoe or pant leg make contact as he stepped over it.

The bar was nearly empty, which he liked. A few Wall Street types laughed at a crude joke. A young couple in a booth leaned across the table and spoke softly. A pair of tourists disagreed on the tip. Larry took a seat at the corner of the bar which was farthest from people.

He ordered a beer and a shot of whiskey. He enjoyed the sting of the shot in his throat and chest. The bartender tried to make small talk which he rebuffed.

Larry was tall and lean, with a crop of thin, gray hair. His face was tight, like plastic wrap stretched too far. Juliana often whispered to her grandfather that his business partner reminded her of a vampire.

After a second shot, Larry's eyes dulled and glossed. He pretended to stare at the Yankees game on the television above the bar. But he was thinking about Joe. He thought about Joe Brescia more than he cared to admit.

Larry and Joe would each admit that their relationship had changed since they lived together in college. Especially since Larry joined BGS about fifteen years ago. A debilitating illness had forced him out of two careers. He had been divorced and miserable. Joe invited him to join the staff as a sales rep. Larry enjoyed immediate success with the young company. After an emergency operation, Larry's health returned and he began to flourish. His fellow employees eventually voted him their representative to the board of directors. Ten years later, he was elected the chairman of the board.

Now, he had a fancy title on his business card and more money than he knew what to do with. But he was miserable.

On the screen, one of the Yankees lined a base hit to right-center. He stood on first and turned to point to his teammates in the dugout. *Joe loved the Yankees.*

Fucking Joe. It was his smile that irritated Larry the most. Who smiles that much? Larry remembered Joe in college – he was more fun back then but just as naive and happy. Everyone wanted to be around him.

Joe is constantly in the paper for saving the world while I am guiding this company to record profits. I made this organization what it is today.

He ordered another shot. As it was being poured, he imagined Joe trying to give a eulogy for him. The people would be as likely to fawn over Joe as they would be to mourn him. Larry saw himself in an open casket, nobody kneeling to pay respects, with Joe encircled by a crowd of his mourners, landing another punchline. His fingers retrieved the coaster from under the beer and folded it methodically before shredding it along the newly creased perforations.

The devil had seen enough. The bartender poured a chianti, smirking under sparking red eyes. Larry's still-smoldering resentment would do just fine.

Larry sipped his beer and decided to act. He took out his phone and made a call while motioning to the bartender for the tab.

"I'm in..."

"Yes..."

"I'm sure..."

"There's only one thing. I need to be the one to tell him."

13

Joe loved the night sky. He took his telescope up to the roof of his building as often as he could. He was old friends with the moon and had been introduced to the planets many times. He met more comets than he could remember and was on a first-name basis with the constellations.

Joe opened his folding chair and took the scope out of its case. He glanced up into the blackness. The unfathomable scale of the universe thrilled him. The sheer distances. The furious beauty of the stars. The destructive creativity of black holes. Color-drenched galaxies stretching *ad infinitum*. And then nothingness – just the emptiness of space for trillions and trillions and billions of trillions of miles.

He extended the tripod and aimed the finderscope at a particular slice of sky. This patch of blackness had been good to him recently so he would return to it tonight. Star-searching was like fishing in that it required patience and repetition.

Joe made a face when he settled into the eyepiece. The city's light pollution was so annoying. He couldn't wait to take Juliana to the country – maybe Maine this summer? There they would have a much brighter sky to fish in.

A little note card was taped to the telescope. It fluttered with every breeze, pulling at the tape like a kid trying to break free of his parent's hand. It had three numbers sharpied on it.

1.4

46,000,000,000

96

They were reminders. Joe always glanced at them before he started scoping. The first referred to an old trick that astronomers used to consider the ridiculous size of VY Canis

MAJORIS, the largest star in the known universe. *Canis Majoris*: 'The Big Dog.' Joe loved this star the most. It was so gargantuan that if the earth were the size of Joe's thumbnail, the corresponding relative diameter of CMA would stretch for 1.4 miles. He looked at his thumb. Canis Majoris was *nine billion* times bigger than the sun. He sighed.

The second number, forty-six billion, was the best guess of the diameter of the known universe - expressed in light years. Light travels at 186,000 miles per second. Joe shook his head. And even more, he remembered, the universe is still expanding! It's constantly growing and stretching at relentless speeds. But that wasn't even the best part - the rate of acceleration of expansion is *still increasing.*

The Big Bang was so powerful that the universe is still emerging from it. He tried to imagine it; *The Big Bang went like this: 'And God said, "Let there be light" and there was light.' Bang.*

The third number, 96, was the percentage of the universe that humanity has not observed yet. We've seen maybe four percent of what's out there. All the knowledge of the universe that humanity had heretofore achieved has been cobbled from this infinitesimally small scrap of a shred of an iota of what is.

"There are two trillion galaxies in the known universe," Joe said to the sky but trailed off. *Two trillion...in the* visible *universe! Each of those galaxies has, say, a hundred million stars, in it. And each of those stars has countless planets. And that doesn't even include the 96 percent of what we haven't seen yet!*

Unreasonable magnitude. Unbearable cerebration. Joe was overcome by an awareness of his own smallness.

And God behind it all. There was something about the unsounded majesty of the universe which inflamed the love of God in his heart. Who can be responsible for such size? God is sometimes shrouded like the blackness of deep space and often just as silent. God is the creator and knower of each galaxy supercluster and hypergiant star, the creator and knower of each quark and atom. Joe believed the universe is so beautiful because God is so beautiful.

The folding chair scraped against the concrete roof as he shifted to get a better angle to the scope. His phone buzzed. It was Ang: *movie?* Joe replied: *on the roof. come up.* Three dots appeared then stopped then came up again: *have fun Galileo*

He retrieved a notepad and pen from the telescope case and placed them on his lap. He dipped a little and eased into the eyepiece, calibrating the settings of the scope without looking up. Joe drew in a crisp breath and asked God to unveil his glory.

14

THURSDAY, APRIL 13

Later that night, the breath in Joe's lungs was removed from him while he slept - slowly and for show, the way magicians pull ribbons from their mouths. Joe shot up, disoriented, suffocating. A pillow tumbled to the floor. Joe sensed that the breath he needed to breathe was *rightthere*, just beyond his mouth and nose. It moved each time he tried to capture it. A bully playing keep-away. Short sounds choked out of his mouth. His vision spangled and faded. After two more tries, he caught the breath or he was allowed it.

He gasped it greedily. He squinted at the alarm clock, heaving, and the bright red numbers eventually told him it was 3:00 am. The darkness in their bedroom was different and thick and heavy. The zeroes on the click blinked. There were red pupils in their center.

There was pressure on Joe's legs. Hot pressure. Then it was on his waist. It slithered up to his chest and pinned his shoulders. He smelled something – leather? raw meat? Joe tried to call out for Angela but the pressure clamped down on his throat. The corners of the pillow fattened as his head was pushed down. He fought it, swinging wildly, trying to get it off his neck. His eyes bulged. Joe's arms flailed and his right hand brushed the crucifix which hung on the wall by his bedside.

He screamed the name of Jesus.

The pressure ceased immediately and the darkness softened. Angela shook him.

"Joe?! Wake up! Wake up! Joseph!"

He felt her hands on his face.

"It's me, bub. Joe. Joe. It's ok. You were having a nightmare. It's alright now."

Joe hurled himself onto her. She held him. He was drenched in sweat. His breath came in ragged gasps.

"It wasn't...I don't think it was...It wasn't a dream." He put his fingertips to his throat, gently tapping on his neck in the dark.

"What happened, bub? I'm here. Tell me about it."

Joe described it but talking about it brought back the dark sensation. He sobbed into her chest, repeating the name of Jesus softly. She assured him that it was only a dream and then held her husband until he fell back asleep.

Angela woke up early to make Joe breakfast in bed. She was relieved to see him sleeping soundly. *Poor guy had a rough night. Never seen him have a nightmare like that before.* She picked up a pillow from the ground near her husband's side and tossed it back on the bed.

15

Nanette Romano walked into the office just before 8 am. She put her coffee on her desk and draped her pocketbook over the back of her chair. Nan was in her office for a full minute before she noticed a pair of legs jutting out behind her desk. She shrieked. Looked again. Joe sat on the ground, his head in his hands. He held a sheet of paper in one hand and a thick manila envelope in the other.

"Joe, you scared me! What are you doing down there?"

He didn't reply. Or look up. Just handed her a letter.

The letterhead announced THE LAW OFFICES OF FERRENCE & SHAW. She knew that firm. They handled the big sexual harassment case last summer, the one with the high-profile big shot who groped just about every young woman in his office. It was in the papers for weeks. Nan's shoulders tensed.

The first few lines of the letter confirmed the sinking feeling in her spirit.

This office has been retained by Victoria D. Rowan pursuant to impending litigation against Joseph F. Brescia III...

Victoria Rowan? *Who the hell was Vic...Tori from Legal?* The letter hung limply in her hand. Nan tried to read the whole thing at once and had to force herself to start slowly from the beginning.

...compulsive, repeated and humiliating acts of sexual harassment, sexual misconduct, unwanted sexual advances, lewd language, creating an unsafe working environment...

She looked at him. Scoured his face. Returned to the letter.

We hereby demand without waiver or prejudice a payment of $15 million dollars for pain, suffering, emotional damage...

Nanette made a short sound. This had to be a joke.

"Wha...Joe, what is this?"

"Some guy served me with papers outside Saint Agnes. Right after Mass."

Nan slunk into her chair, asking herself if Joe could have done this. They sat in silence for many moments, she and Joe and the letter and their questions. If someone had been assaulted then justice must be done. No matter who it was. She knew Joe. At least, she thought she knew him...No.

Nanette decided that these accusations were false.

Joe finally spoke. "You believe me, right?"

She replied in her no-nonsense way. "Don't ever ask me that again."

He allowed himself a brief smile.

The more she thought about it, the more she dismissed the possibility that the allegations were true or even partially true. Joe was a gentleman. Hundreds – maybe thousands – of people would attest to that. He was happily married. This conduct was not possible for Joe, much less to the degrees of depravity spelled out in the letter. She regretted even considering that he was guilty.

"Thanks, Nan. What do you think this is? Why would she do this?"

Nanette thought back to the handful of times she had interacted with Tori. The girl turned heads wherever she went. That long red hair was a frequent topic of conversation in the building. But there was something off about her

Nan vaguely remembered Tori glowering at Joe a few times. *Why didn't I say anything?*

"It's gotta be a money grab. Right?"

Joe stared at the coffee mug on her desk.

"Did you have any interactions with her that were out of place? I have to tell you, I noticed her a few times staring in your direction with a weird look on her face. I'm sorry I didn't say anything."

"It's OK. I know what you are talking about. I'm sorry I didn't say anything to you either. A few times she said some aggressive things to me. She came up to me at the Christmas party. We were talking, no big deal, but I caught a look in her eye. She kinda bit her lip and said we should go for a walk. I'm pretty sure I knew what she meant so I said goodbye and walked away. Angela was 10 feet away talking to someone! Since then she's been weird with me. I told Ang about it. She said something weird to Juliana the other day, too."

Nan chewed her lip, trying to make sense of it all.

"So she had a crush on you. You rejected her advances. Fine, that happens. But to take it to this extreme?

"Angela says she's obsessed and she would do something like this. She called it. Shit, Ang. Let me call her. I don't want her to see this on the news before she hears it from me. You call my attorneys and get them down here. And I want to address the whole company in five minutes."

The latter idea proved unfeasible.

They each reached for a phone and started the preemptive process of clearing Joe's name. Nan's phone rang as she reached to pick it up. They looked at each other. The caller ID said TELECOM MEDIA.

"Joseph Brescia's office," she answered with none of her usual cheer.

"Yes." The voice on the other end of the phone seemed relieved he had gotten through. "Um, yes, this is Dylan from CelebrityTrash.com. Can I speak to Mr. Brescia?"

With the phone to her ear, she nodded at Joe. It had begun.

"He isn't available right now. What is this in reference to?"

"We wanted to give Mr. Brescia a chance to go on the record about sexually harassing his employee. I mean *allegedly*. He allegedly sexually harassed his employee. Does he have anything to say? Also - we want him to come to our studios for an exclusive on-camera interview."

The story was out. Tori's lawyers must have tipped off the press. Nan opened the local news sites. One by one, from the most reputable to the least, they had a story about Joe somewhere on their front page. She checked the major news outlets next. Most of them had it. Nan's phone rang again. It didn't stop ringing. One by one, the red lights on Nan's desk phone lit up with voicemails. Email requests for interviews surged in four and five at a time.

Everyone in the media wanted to be the first to talk to Joe. It seemed he was the latest wealthy pervert whose crimes had caught up to him. The story wrote itself for the tabloids, blogs and television shows: squeaky clean CEO and philanthropist actually a miscreant who is undone by lascivious crimes against a sexy employee.

Thirty-eight floors below, several news trucks competed for the space closest to the door of the building. A horde of reporters jostled on the sidewalk outside the property at 1119 Lexington Avenue. Joe Brescia would have to come out sometime. Producers and camera crews set to work framing their shots and angling for light. Everyone in the media busied themselves for Joe's emergence except one woman in the crowd. She looked the part but nobody noticed that she wasn't affiliated with any station or paper. She alone was still amidst the tumult. The woman's eyes burned a violent red and a thin sneer widened the corners of her mouth.

Across the country, people beginning their day came across the story on television or online. It even led some of the morning talk shows. They read about Joe on their phones while on the train or in line for a bagel. If they didn't know him before, the world was now at least peripherally aware of Joseph Brescia. Those who knew Joe were appalled that he was accused of these things. Most folks encountering the story had no rooting interest except that they disliked all the bad guys in the news; velvet villains who abuse their hard-working employees. They subconsciously categorized Joe alongside the corrupt and perverted who inhabit the world's corporate boardrooms, political offices and country clubs.

Forty minutes later, Eli Morgan summoned the courage to knock on the doors of the big conference room. The staff at BGS – from the most senior board member to the most inexperienced intern – were blindsided by the news. Joe's employees and Tori's co-workers heard the news for the first time along with the rest of the country.

Eli had been tracking the developments on his phone and computer. He was hurt that BGS was in the news for the wrong reason. He was furious that his boss was being maligned by every media outlet before being given a chance to defend himself. But Eli was most disturbed by his co-workers' reaction to the story. He wasn't brave enough to declare it but he believed that Joe was innocent. At the very least, he reasoned, people should give Joe the benefit of the doubt or wait until the proceedings played out in court. Instead they condemned him as guilty this morning and would do their best to have him executed in the court of public opinion on their primetime shows and happy hours that evening.

Eli stepped into the room and tried a brave face. There were a dozen people inside. No one noticed him come in. Four men Eli had only seen pictures of on the company website conferred to his left. On his right and nearer, a woman whom he knew worked for Joe's legal counsel – he once split a cab with her – huddled with Larry Denham, the chairman of the BGS board of directors. He wasn't eavesdropping but he heard her say *80-20 against* and *too late for that*. When Larry saw Eli, he motioned her to lower her voice.

There in the center of the room was Joe.

His face was buried in his wife's shoulder, his nose poking out through her dark hair. They weren't really hugging – more like she was holding him. Eli had never seen Joe nervous, much less like this.

"Mr. Brescia...I'm sorry to bother you." A few heads turned to Eli then resumed their business. Joe stood up from Angela's embrace and faced Eli. He looked Joe in the eyes. "Mr. Brescia, I want you to know that I support you. I don't think you did this."

Joe's face was scarlet. Angela clasped her husband's left hand with both of hers, thumbs tenderly tracing circles on his wrist. She looked up at Eli, her eyes telling him *thanks*. More attorneys poured into the room. They opened briefcases and cleared space on the big mahogany conference table. One of them leaned over and whispered to Joe that they needed to begin.

"I can't tell you how much that means to me, El. Let me ask you – what are the folks in the office saying? How bad is it out there?"

The attorney whispered again, this time glancing at Eli with noticeable agitation.

Eli looked at the floor. Joe Brescia had never asked anything of him, not to get him a cup of coffee or to know the time. Now, the scandalized CEO wanted Eli to gauge the social temperature of his employees. Rumors confirming Joe's guilt had already started to circulate through the 38th floor of the building.

"Just say it, Eli. It's ok," Angela encouraged him.

Eli stammered. One of the attorneys guided Eli outside the room. He turned around when he heard the pleading in Joe's voice.

"Elijah. Tell me. Please."

Eli swallowed, looked at them and spoke the truth. "It's bad Mr. B. It's very bad out there."

16

Brescia Accused of Sexual Harassment by Employee; Embroiled in $15 Million Lawsuit

By Millie Keefe
Daily Sentinel reporter

Joseph Brescia, the highly regarded CEO of Brescia Global Solutions, is at the center of a sexual harassment scandal. The former City Councilman, 63, is accused of abusive behavior by Tori Rowan, a 30-year-old paralegal. Leaked copies of the affidavit reveal a laundry list of alleged sexual misconduct including groping, requests for oral sex, stalking and intimidation in the office.

The lawsuit was announced by Rowan's attorneys, the firm of Ferrence & Shaw, at a press conference yesterday. She is suing Brescia for $15 million.

Rowan says through her lawyers that Brescia's alleged harassment began after she spurned his advances at a company Christmas party last year. She states that she was fearful for her job and for her life when Brescia became more aggressive in recent weeks.

Ms. Rowan remained silent during the 30-minute press conference. She dabbed her eyes as some of the more explicit allegations were read.

As details of the accusations continue to emerge, a massive public outcry has grown on behalf of Mr. Brescia. Supporters of the New Haven, CT native have pointed to his pristine reputation and a lengthy list of charitable accomplishments. Brescia's harshest critics cite a long line of debased public figures who used outward altruism to mask private misconduct.

A divided public remains mesmerized by the scandal.

Brescia has been married to his wife Angela for 39 years. They have one son and one granddaughter. Brescia was a lieutenant in the Air Force before founding Brescia Global Solutions, the world's leading supplier of aerospace security technologies in 1996. BGS recorded $390 million in profit last year.

COMMENTS SECTION | YOU MUST BE A REGISTERED USER TO COMMENT, ALL COMMENTS ARE SUBJECT TO THE DAILY SENTINEL SUBMISSION GUIDELINES

Joeybaggadonuts: another fat cat scumbag gets what he derserves!

TopRuth: the courts should put him away for life so he can't do this to anyone else.

Lenny Smalls: he's stealing second!

rightandrong: He though power and entitlement made him exempt from the law. Poor girl!

tristanX: I never thought Joe Brescia would do something like this. He seems like the nicest guy! Just goes to show anyone can be a pervert no matter how generous they appear to be.

PCFriar2006: I knew this guy in college. Him and his buddies thought they were the coolest, hanging out all day laughing and joking about stuff like this.

Fortuneforglory: He'll get his in prison :-)

KiK&Tim: "Alleged" mean anything to anyone these days?

Mark3446: Your family should be ashamed of you Brescia. You call yourself a Christian? Jesus is ashamed of you. There's a special place in hell for scum like you.

CINCYeven: sucks to be you Joe.

NEXT | PAGE 1 OF 91| LAST

17

Joe's knees ached from the stone floor. The church was empty except Joe and the hundreds of angels worshipping in silence alongside him.

Earlier at the office, Joe spent hours listening to his attorneys and publicists. They were as indignant as Joe about the false accusations but they advised him to say nothing to the media as they planned their countersuits. *You will have your day in court...the truth will come out*, they cautioned. Joe rejected that. During one of their speeches, Joe walked out of the conference room and exited the building.

The reporters gathered outside were shocked to see him come out, especially without a retinue of handlers, lawyers, PR spinsters and advisers. Usually the disgraced corporate types hole themselves up in an office or penthouse and try to wait out the media before giving a somber, I-have-soul-searching-to-do interview. The journalists were even more surprised to see Joe speak candidly without a prepared statement.

Protestors, demonstrators and activists lined up across the street from the media staging area. They held signs that read **JUSTICE FOR TORI** and **BOYS WILL BE ~~BOYS~~ HELD ACCOUNTABLE**.

He motioned for the demonstrators across the street to come over. The cops held down the caution tape and stopped traffic to let them cross the street. Joe wanted everyone to hear what he had to say. He spoke emotionally and honestly. Here in the quiet of the church, he replayed those words in his mind.

"I'm not afraid to tell you all that I am innocent. I don't need a script to tell the truth. I have nothing to hide. I didn't do this or anything like this."

When he had finished, the media clamored for more quotes and more emotion. They shouted follow-up questions and shoved their microphones in front of his mouth, hoping for more of this unprecedented spontaneity.

He declined and started walking. Joe didn't have a plan. His feet more or less guided him to Saint Agnes. The walk to the church was brutal. The paparazzi hounded him. Protestors screamed ugly things. He struggled to get through them to the doors of the church. They did not follow him inside. Outside he tried to be as serene as possible. Now, on his knees in the soothing silence, he was raw and emotional. The façade of calm vanished and he gave Jesus the deep things of his heart — anguish, despair and confusion.

He rubbed his temples, as if trying to loosen the memory which would explain all this. Did Joe commit some secret sin for which he was now being punished? For an instant, Joe considered the possibility that he was, in fact, guilty of these crimes but somehow had repelled them from his memory. Nothing came to mind. His conscience was clear. This gave Joe a moment's peace.

Joe's guardian angel knelt beside him and whispered in his ear.

Joe had an inspiration. He abruptly changed the direction and theme of his prayers. His posture became more upright. His hands unclasped and he lifted them above his head. He stopped praying for guidance, clarity and protection and started audibly praising God.

"Lord God... You know I'm innocent and I know I'm innocent. The rest is up to you. Do with me what you will. Praise you, God!"

Satan stood at the back of the church, leaning against the confessional. He had been observing Joe for the last hour. The devil was not pleased that Joe was here honoring God in silence rather than seeking comfort from people. And Satan absolutely hated that Joe changed his prayers from asking to thanking, from supplication to appreciation.

The devil nodded slowly in assent, as if acknowledging that the first round went to Joe. He didn't expect Joe to forsake the faith he had spent a lifetime cultivating on the first attack but he had not expected this. The devil sneered, his ego bruised by Joe's joy. Satan glared at the multitude of angels. They were praying passionately for Joe and Joe's guardian angel. They ignored the devil. This infuriated him as much as Joe's humble prayer. He spoke loudly so the angels could hear him.

"You all better pray." The devil looked at Joe. He despised him. "You better pray real hard because I have not even *begun* to go to work on him."

18

The airport throbbed with activity. So many people on a mission to hurry up and wait.

The young man with the shaggy blonde hair was about 25. He had some fuzz on his chin and wore a white long-sleeved t-shirt and jeans. He carried a backpack and a laptop bag. He looked like your neighbor's son, the one who came inside to drink your orange juice after playing basketball in your driveway. Or the guy your daughter dated for a semester in college. He worked the cash register at your grocery store, delivered your pizza and asked if you wanted the large popcorn for only 50 cents more.

He certainly didn't look like the leader and champion of a cause which was birthed in protest, raised in dispute and was now ready to die in violence. That was the beauty of their cause; they came from everywhere. He wondered if the media would refer to him as a "terrorist" tomorrow. Or a "domestic terrorist" because he was from here? He envisioned the headlines and what photo they would use. Probably the one from his Twitter.

Today was the long-awaited day, the day they would announce themselves to the world. He looked everywhere around the busy screening area except in the direction of his accomplice pretending to do her security job a few yards away. He tried to distract himself by reading the signs in the airport. Exit this way to taxis and the street; various terminals and gates marked by arrows; customs just down this corridor. He read each letter and word carefully to keep his mind occupied. He almost burst out laughing when he happened upon a TSA warning sign:

Explosives and firearms prohibited.

Too funny. If they only knew what he had in his laptop bag.

The rush of excitement and fear caused him a moment of dizziness. How come in the movies the bad guy is always so chill? He was ashamed of being nervous. He tried to project a suave indifference.

The line to go through the metal detectors moved slowly. He counted the people waiting ahead of him: 21. A teenage boy who was devastated to be traveling with his parents. Three college-aged girls who were dressed as though for bed. Two couples: the men bald, the women obese, though they prided themselves on every wrist-tracked step. Five middle-aged men named Alan who sold software. A pudgy guy with long hair and a Darth Vader t-shirt. Five twenty-something dudes – total bros. They were basically the same person: tank tops, basketball shorts, high socks, sneakers, one earbud in, one dangling over the other ear, backwards hats. *They think of nothing but their biceps and their one-night stands. These are the ones whose deaths delight me the most.*

He wondered if any of these folks would be on his plane. He hoped at least the frat bros were. What do people do if they know they are going to die – say goodbye to mom and fake some prayers? But no, these living pit stains were laughing and talking about how hot Amber's friends were last night.

"All belts, all shoes and all jackets come off. Laptops come out of the bag and in their own bin. Everything out of your pockets. Not even a tissue," a blue agent declared. Again.

The people who weren't on his plane would be awed when they eventually realized they waited in the security line with him. In a few days, when they pieced together the details, they would natter about how close they were to death. He hated them, all of them. The more the news covered his work, the more these sheep would feel as if they accomplished something just by being here. They would solemnly declare some bullshit about being "blessed" or "lucky." Being spared that day must have been "God's will" and they were "fortunate to be alive." Or his favorite: "It could have been me on that plane with him."

Behind him, at a little coffee shop, a line of pre-caffeinated zombies lurched forward obediently, retrieving lattes and cappuccinos, every time an order was called. A human suit paced near the entrance to the queue like he was guarding it, gesturing and proclaiming to some *Brad* in an earpiece that the fiscal year wasn't over yet and they could still finish strong. Ahead of him, a TSA agent asked everyone *hihowahya* as he took boarding passes but bent his head and didn't care about the response. To his right, a mother and two daughters compared the charms on their bracelets. The tinty spangling caught in his ear. At his left, a father scowled into his phone and scrolled through the pictures his daughter posted last night. A businesswoman hoisted a purse over one shoulder and a big bag over another. Why did she need two bags? It was just too much. They were all of one sheeply mind. All of them. Their conformity to their shimmering culture disgusted him. Too bad he couldn't take them all. Lemmings.

A few places ahead of him in line was a teenage girl he had not counted earlier. She had headphones on, those big headphones.

Maybe 19 or 20. Brown hair fell in bulky bangs over her forehead, but in a kind of cool, curvy way. She wore a tight green t-shirt that had the logo of a vintage soda company on it and a flowery skirt. Long legs. Her belly button was visible in between where her shirt ended and her skirt began. She had a backpack on. It was covered in pins. She seemed to be by herself.

The green t-shirt was a little damp in the back. There was a little sweat building on her lower back and along her neck.

The sweat on her skin excited him. He turned his head subtly to get a better look. The bustle of the airport provided perfect cover. She would never know. Plus, he knew how to look without being caught.

She stood there, listening to music, waiting in line. Oblivious.

He averted his eyes and locked them onto the floor when she happened to glance in his direction. He waited a moment and then closed his eyes to further orchestrate the scene in his mind, his feet shuffling ahead when the line moved.

The women that separated him and the teenage girl split off to another x-ray line and now he and the girl in the green t-shirt stood next to each other. He looked away, looked back. Mouth dry. Mind racing. Heart racing. Should he say something? He wanted to kiss her. At least talk to her.

His accomplice was sweating, also, through her TSA uniform. She was desperately trying to get the terrorist's attention but he was in his own world. From her position behind the controls of the x-ray machine, the accomplice kept trying to make eye contact with him. He was only a few places away from the machine but had a far-off look in his eye. He was probably thinking about his impending death, she realized. *Such a dreamer.* There was too much at stake right now to be philosophizing about life and death.

In a few moments, she would override the x-ray's warning functionality and let him and his laden laptop through to the plane. They had been working to perfect the details for so long. Why wasn't he focused, now of all times?

The accomplice's heart thudded so hard that she was certain her co-workers at the airport were onto them. What if the override program didn't work? She tried to breathe down the adrenaline.

The young man with the shaggy blonde hair absentmindedly scratched the stubble on his chin.

Come on, look up! You're almost at the conveyor belt!

The passengers ahead of him removed their shoes and belts and he snapped back to his senses. He took off his shoes and belt and placed them along with his wallet and cell phone in one of the hard plastic bins. He handed one of the bins to a teenage girl in a green t-shirt as she put headphones into her backpack. The girl thanked him. The accomplice exhaled a sigh of relief. OK, he was back now.

He hefted his carry-on onto the conveyor belt and took the laptop out of its bag and put it in its own bin. Jolts of anticipation shot through him as he pushed it toward the x-ray machine. When his items were next to be scanned, she keyed in the algorithm their tech team had spent five years developing. She thought about all the time spent infiltrating this shitty job. This was it.

They forgot to breathe.

The laptop bag went through the x-ray machine unceremoniously and plopped onto the rollers on the other side.

They each exhaled. He went through the scanner without incident.

He hastily grabbed the laptop and put it back in its bag, then put his shoes on. Slip-on loafers, no laces - it was faster. He had planned every detail. He even packed things that would make it seem like he was going away for the weekend if anyone asked or wanted to look.

He looked back over his shoulder and made eye contact with his accomplice. She suppressed a smile and resumed her work.

Goodbye, my love. They said it this morning. There were more important things to do now.

He started walking toward the terminal. *It was too easy.*

He stopped and turned around at the sound of a voice.

"You forgot your belt." The pretty girl with the green t-shirt and the big headphones. The headphones were now draped around her neck. She was holding his belt out toward him.

He stammered. He had to say something now. This had to be a sign. He wanted to kiss her.

"You might need that," she laughed. He put the laptop bag down on top of his backpack and hastily fed the belt through the loops of his jeans. She continued toward her terminal. He hustled a few steps to catch up with her, still buckling his belt.

The laptop bag rested precipitously, unattended.

"Hey, hold up. I didn't get to thank you."

The accomplice watched them. She was heartbroken, not because of the girl – he always cheated on her – but because he could not stay focused. So committed to the cause but so easily distracted.

The bros emerged from the security checkpoint, joking about how the TSA screeners can see you naked. As they walked past, laughing and looking for the bar, one of them accidentally kicked the backpack on which the laptop bag rested. It toppled to the floor.

Shit.

He whirled around. The accomplice saw it too. For an instant, they winced and waited for it to explode. It didn't. He forgot about the girl.

When he realized it didn't go off, he uncurled his arms from around his head and face. The instinctive gesture betrayed him - nobody reacts to a fallen laptop like there was a bomb in it.

He bent to scoop it up but paused. He needed to get the laptop on the plane. He needed to think. He hesitated to touch it. There was no time and no privacy.

All the eyes in the immediate vicinity turned to him. Did he cry out and not know it? Suddenly he could not catch his breath. One of the frat bros stooped to retrieve the laptop bag for him.

"Don't fucking touch it!" His voice was high and desperate.

The girl in the green t-shirt and the frat bros stared at him, mouths slightly open. Dozens of people in the area stopped and turned to him. A hush replaced the usual buzz.

Two officers stationed nearby moved immediately toward him. Both had automatic weapons strapped over the front of their vests. One held the leash of a German shepherd who had been lying patiently at his officer's feet. The dog's ears perked up at the sound of the scream.

The young man had recovered his belongings but not his poise. Too many eyes on him. He was almost hyperventilating as the officers moved to either side of him. The dog strained at his leash.

He was holding the laptop bag out in front of him like a pizza box instead of utilizing the strap.

The accomplice averted her eyes. Abort.

Fuck.

The dog aggressively sniffed him and his bags. The crowd stopped to watch with muted solemnity.

"Everything OK here sir?" One officer addressed him, the other subtly communicated the situation up the ladder via a small radio on his shoulder.

"Yes, sir. Of course, sir."

"What's in the bag?"

"Nothing. I just get a little nervous about flying. Thanks officers."

The guards studied him. His breathing was off. So much sweat. They didn't believe him.

The dog growled and barked at the laptop bag,

He knew it was over. He lunged and tried to unzip the bag.

The scuffle was over in five seconds. The officers separated him from the laptop bag. One of them pinned him to the ground. The dog snarled.

A team of security personnel arrived and assisted in the arrest. They pushed the stunned crowd back and sequestered the area. The commotion was over in moments.

The accomplice faded into the crowd and considered how much time she had before he gave her up to the authorities.

19

Brazen Terrorist Nearly Gets Homemade Bomb on Plane; TSA "Shocked" by Faulty X-Ray Machine

By Millie Keefe
Daily Sentinel reporter

Tragedy was averted Thursday at LaGuardia when a team of officers including a bomb-sniffing police dog discovered a passenger who had made it through security carrying homemade explosives embedded in a laptop. Federal officials believe a faulty x-ray machine allowed the attacker to nearly board a flight for Las Vegas. No details have been released regarding the identity, motive or affiliation of the perpetrator.

Brescia Global Solutions, whose founder and CEO Joseph Brescia is currently involved in a high-profile sexual harassment lawsuit, has been branded as responsible for the close call by several government officials. State Senator Chris Rodriguez has been the most vocal of those castigating the makers of the x-ray equipment.

"Brescia Global Solutions has let us all down," Rodriguez said. "The investigation is not yet complete but it's safe to say I'm shocked at their negligence. This machine's malfunction almost caused the loss of life. Luckily, our officers were in a position to defend the American people when BGS was not. I will immediately recommend a comprehensive review of our security partners. All New Yorkers, all Americans and all people who use these airports deserve better."

Each of New York's 19 airports uses BGS equipment.

Joseph Brescia was not immediately available for comment.

COMMENTS SECTION|YOU MUST BE A REGISTERED USER TO COMMENT, ALL COMMENTS ARE SUBJECT TO THE DAILY SENTINEL SUBMISSION GUIDELINES

baldr.dash: I love how karma comes around. If you live like an @ssh*le it will always come back to get you.

tONY54: give a man to fish, he eats for a day. teach a man to fish, he eats for the rest of his life

lockload88: first bresia rapes that girl and now he doesn't have the stones to answer for this. real class act.

LJJoolie: I worked for joe, best job i ever had

Trindo: When it's not your week, it is really not your week. #worstweekeverforbrescia

Klimm1: This is why I dontr fly anymore. You cant trust anyone. Anyone can be a terrorist these days.

Rolee: what does Brescia being accused of harassment have anything to do with the malfunction? They are NOT related. People are piling on this guy.

Armando: Nice work boys. AMERICA: land of the free, home of the brave, baby.

Tujj: im just glad no one got hurt. Lesson learned. Lets get BGS out of there and someone else in charge of our nations security. Im not flying any airport that uses them. They cant be trusted with that f$&k running things.

NEXT | PAGE 1 OF 229| LAST

20

FRIDAY, APRIL 14

The throng of reporters waiting for him had doubled in size and fervor. The incident at the airport was front-page news throughout the country. As Joe approached his office building, the media horde started toward him, microphones outstretched and cameras rolling.

"Joe – what do you have to say about your company's negligence nearly contributing to a terrorist attack?

"What is BGS going to do to prevent this in the future? Are you going to resign?"

"What's worse, almost letting your country down or being accused of sexual harassment?"

He drew in a quick breath, locked eyes with the nearest reporter and brusquely told her that he was investigating the incident himself. He asked them to wait for all the facts before assigning blame. He picked out snippets of phrases amid the shouting but his head snapped to the right when he heard Juliana's name. Joe couldn't see who said it though he looked them all over several times.

He left their incessant, damning questions in the spectacular sunshine and entered the cool marble lobby. Two security guards stood to greet Joe. These guards were among the people who didn't like seeing his name trashed two ways. Joe greeted them briskly and kept moving. He thought of Juliana on the elevator ride up. He asked God to shield her from the media's coverage of both stories. She would be devastated.

Joe entered the BGS offices and felt 29 pairs of eyes on him. The employees were split on their loyalty to Joe but all of them were astonished to see him show up to work on time. He stopped at Nan's desk and she stood to embrace him with a firm hug. She quickly ascertained how badly he was enduring the onslaught of scrutiny.

"Joe...maybe you should take a few days..."

He shook his head summarily as if he had already considered the thought and rejected it. She knew better than to force the issue – she had more pressing matters to present to him.

"OK, well, then here's what we have going on... Larry and two reps from the board are in your office right now. They've been here since 7:45 waiting for you. Our Incident Review Team is flying in; with traffic, they'll be here, say 9:45, 10. Investigators from the FAA are coming at 11. They asked for a few hours and I know they're the top priority right now so I cleared your whole afternoon. The investors we had lined up for lunch today were not happy about that. I told them we'll make it up to them. Remember we have the reps from Hong Kong in town all next week also so you would have to decide who we want to piss off less. And, alright, let's see, we got calls from the terminal expansion projects in New Orleans and Dallas. I'm sorry but they're both out. I know how much we wanted them. Already looking into flights for you, I figured you would want to go out there and work your magic in person. Both cities in two days - next week? It would be crazy but it could work. Denver wants to video-conference with us right away, today, if possible, but I told them tomorrow. Monday at the latest. It doesn't look good with them, either. Sorry. The governor and the mayor's office have, like, five different departments calling to schedule a sit down with us. I think we should just do them all at once instead of one at a time; one meeting for the state, one for the city. The airlines all called; they're all panicking as you might expect. I told them we'll reach out next week."

She took a deep breath.

"OK, then, tonight, I scheduled the legal teams for 7 in the conference room. I'll get some dinner and snacks up there for you all. It's probably going to be a late night. Our counsel has all their people working on the, um, lawsuit so they brought in new people to start working on the airport situation. Trying to get some more workspaces set up and connected for all of them. The detectives working the case at the airport already came and left. They'll be back but they didn't say when. They're probably trying to talk to you before the FBI and Homeland Security start throwing their weight around. Both of them, by the way, want you in their offices tomorrow. I don't know how I'm going to get you there yet because tomorrow O'Hare and LAX are both sending people here. I have cars lined up to get them at the airport because I know how important they are for us. I cancelled the Systems Integration conference call. Deal with that later. I have all these meetings staggered so you can take a break in between."

When Nan finished, Joe looked unsteady on his feet.

"I know it's a lot." She glanced at her computer. Four more emails had come in while she was speaking. It was 8:09 am.

"Are you alright, Joe?"

He didn't respond but put one hand on the doorknob. Joe seemed to stare at it. Then he closed his eyes. Nan knew he was praying. Seated behind her desk, she closed her eyes and joined him.

"Don't let them take what you've built," Nan said with urgency. She had meant to say it softly and surprised herself. He looked back at her without saying anything. His face was hard, set like flint. Joe opened the door and walked into his office.

21

Three men in sharp suits did not stand to greet him. They lounged comfortably on the plush chairs and sofa in his office. Joe strode past them to his desk and sat down. Larry clicked the top of his pen several times, studying Joe. A stubborn silence filled the space between them.

"You have a major problem," Larry finally began. "Two of them, actually. Either one of them would be enough for the board to call for drastic action."

"And what is the board calling for?"

Despite his long friendship with Joe, Larry knew the rest of the board of directors had been trying to wrest controlling interest in the company from Joe for years. Larry was the fulcrum, fluctuating between the pressure of his colleagues and loyalty to his friend. Both Joe and Larry knew this turmoil would be the best opportunity the board would ever have to oust him. The chill between them indicated as much.

One of the other men began to speak but Larry glared him into silence then continued. Larry's voice had a tone of both menace and pleading.

"You have an opportunity to walk away from all this quietly, Joe. You can save it from getting worse. Cut your losses and let us clean up your...this...mess."

Joe looked at Larry sadly, painfully. He no longer saw an old friend; this was now a rival contending for his title.

"My mess?"

"Yes Joe, your mess. Or have you not been following the news lately?" Larry sat back, crossed one leg over the other and folded his arms.

"Oh, I've been following it, Larry. The news and the talk shows and the table. They're feasting on me. Yes, old friend, I've heard them all. What I haven't heard, though, is a peep from you or the board. Not a single word on my behalf."

Joe exhaled and made a triangle on the desk with his elbows and fingertips.

"I didn't harass anyone and we don't know the cause of the malfunction at the airport."

"You want sympathy from us, Joe? You want a sweet statement about some orphanage you built? This could fucking ruin us. Not to mention that there are others who sit at our table who tend to believe Tori."

One of the other men in Joe's office blurted out "Joe, we have voted to suspend you. Indefinitely. No appeal."

Larry whirled around, chin askew and eyes fierce. Larry wasn't sure if he wanted to be the one to deliver the death blow because he was the closest to Joe or because he had the most resentment for him. Either way, Larry should have been the one to tell him.

A rising flume of anger welled up within Joe and he weighed the consequences of acting on it. Whether the board believed he was guilty or whether they wanted to use it as leverage against him was irrelevant. These men were once his friends and business partners. They had eaten at his table, with his family.

"Joe," Larry started but Joe waved him off. Joe's chin trembled.

Larry had betrayed him. All that they achieved together, all that Joe did for him over the years counted for nothing.

Joe Brescia felt overwhelmingly alone.

He refused to express any emotion in front of them. Without a word, he reached his left hand down to open a desk drawer. With a sharp movement, he leaned over and grabbed something. Something heavy. The three men half-stood. Did Joe keep a weapon in that drawer?

"Joe – wait."

He tossed the leather photo album on his desk. It landed with a thud. The men sat back down. Joe aggressively flipped through the pages. He found the picture he wanted and slid his hand under the plastic. Joe stared at it, unconcerned with the awkward shifting of the men in his office. Memories bubbled to the surface of his mind.

Larry knew exactly what photo Joe held.

Joe stood and walked towards the door, leaving the album open on his desk. Before he left, he dropped the photo on Larry's lap. He did not say a word.

The board member in the room who had not said anything during the exchange shriveled his lips into the slightest sneer before resuming a more hardened expression. His pupils reddened.

Once clear of his office, tears formed in Joe's eyes. Head down, he went directly to the men's room. He had to clear his mind before the FAA investigators arrived to interrogate him. Too much to think about. Each lie, each smear felt like an emotional lash from an unseen whip wielded by some malicious tormenter. He sat in a stall and wept. In a moment of despair, Joe did not necessarily want to die but he did not necessarily want to continue living.

Back in Joe's office, Larry couldn't look at the picture. He moved his head so his eyes could not glance at it. *This is what it takes to get to the top, Larry.*

Larry walked out. The picture fluttered to the floor. The other two board members called him but he ignored them. One stooped to pick up the photo.

In it, Larry and Joe smiled from adjacent hospital beds. They looked about twenty years younger. Both wore hospital gowns. Despite the toll of major surgeries, they each displayed big grins and flashed four thumbs up. It was taken the morning after the emergency transplant operation which Joe volunteered for, the one that saved Larry's life.

22

That night, Joe lay on the couch in their living room. Angela cradled his head in her lap. The television was on but muted. They had not spoken for some time. Their questions were too big, answers too rare. Ang played with his hair. Joe felt a surge of gratitude for his wife's devotion. He pulled her face down into his and kissed her.

"Thank you for being with me through this. And trusting me."

She smiled down at him and continued stroking his hair.

"I haven't even asked you how you're doing with everything. You OK?"

"I'm not good, Joe. I'm watching everything they're saying about you. I know we said we were going to ignore everything but I just can't. I read every article and then I read every comment of every article. I hate what they're saying about you. Especially everything that girl is saying, Joe. I *knew* it. I knew she was going to pull something."

"You did, you said it." He spoke to the ceiling.

"I actually went to the roof the other night. Sat out there in your chair."

"Oh, yeah?

"I know how it has always been a place of comfort for you. Thought I'd see if it could do the same for me." His fingers sought hers.

"And?"

"It was nice. Chilly. I don't think it worked. I don't know if I did it right."

"What – praying?" She nodded affirmatively, which he felt but did not see. He swallowed then spoke carefully.

"I don't think there's a right way to do it. People in relationships have intimate conversations, right? I think that's all it is. You just talk with God. Just be real. No fake altar-boy seriousness. You just be your real self. And he'll be his real self. And then when you're done, you listen and God talks. Back and forth, back and forth like that. Sometimes he speaks with words but usually with feelings or impressions or people or things that happen. And then after a while neither of you need words. You just know each other."

"You make it sound so easy." This was not the first time they had this conversation.

"I don't think it's supposed to be complicated."

"Yeah, but I don't know what to say."

"Then I think you start by telling God that you don't know what to say. Then you've already begun. But seriously, I think it's great that you're trying again."

She rubbed her eyes with her palms. He didn't push it.

"Babe, again, I am so grateful for you during all of this. Thank you."

"You can make it up to me some other time," she winked at him. He tried to grin.

"I'm going to get some ice cream," Angela said, rising. He lifted his head so she could get up. "You want anything?"

"Nah. Actually, I think I would like to be alone for a little while."

She poked her head out from behind the freezer door, nodding as if she had expected that. "I'll be out here."

Joe retreated to their bedroom and closed the door behind him. He kicked his shoes off and pulled out a pair of sweats from the drawer. His wallet and keys went on top of the dresser, underneath the new canvas they hung last month. Angela did a watercolor interpretation of VY Canis Majoris as a present for his birthday.

As Joe was getting changed, his eyes took in the crucifix next to his bed. A little ping in his conscience suggested he should pray about everything that was going on. He resisted it. He was so. Didn't feel like praying.

Joe's guardian angel reminded him, with intellectual nudges, that he couldn't fix himself and that he should give all these things to God. Joe eyed the remote control and told himself he would pray tomorrow. The guardian decided to be more insistent and speak to him with words. These registered in Joe's soul as emotional impulses, a flicker of desire. The angel said: *Joseph, your Savior waits for you in the silence of prayer. He waits in your pain, in your confusion. Go there. Allow the Lord Jesus to console you and minister to you. Ease his all-consuming desire to love you. Go to the Cross and unite your sufferings to his. Go to his Cross, Joseph.*

It still had to be chosen, though. Human free will was sacrosanct. Joe looked again at the remote control and again at the crucifix and decided to pray for 10 minutes. He pulled on his favorite hoodie and, sighing, knelt in front of the crucifix.

"In the name of the Father and of the Son and of the Holy Spirit." He could barely keep his eyes open so he asked for the strength to pray.

"Holy guardian angel, please help me."

Joe's guardian angel knelt behind him and fervently asked God that Joe might have the grace to pray well during this meditation. The guardian extended his wings around Joe so that they encircled him snugly and wrapped back around the guardian as well. It was a loving embrace. From this posture, the guardian could pray with Joe while ensuring that he would be safe from any demonic activity that might target him.

Joe took a deep, satisfying breath and actually felt peaceful, like a space of light opened up in the cloud of anguish in his mind. The other morning at Mass, Father Jack preached about using your imagination to let the Holy Spirit guide you in prayer. Joe opened his eyes. The crucifix again.

"Come, Holy Spirit. Help me to pray."

The guardian prostrated himself as the Holy Spirit descended into the room.

The cross was made of brass, the corpus was gold. Maybe eight inches long. Joe gazed on it. He closed his eyes, yawned, and drew another deep breath as he began to meditate on the death of Jesus. He allowed his thoughts to drift and the room around him faded gently from the forefront of his consciousness.

Joe is there in the crowd. He is wearing a dark tunic. His hair is wild without its gel. The crowd is too thick and too rowdy so Joe has no choice but to follow where they lead.

The tumult calms and, for an instant, Joe sees clear through the thicket of limbs and robes. He glimpses Jesus, who glimpses him.

Jesus is beaten beyond description. The gory public scourging leaves his back in bloody ribbons. Joe winces. He knows it is only going to get worse and looks away. When he regains his courage to glance again, he finds Jesus still gazing at him in the little tunnel of vision which has connected them through the din.

A vicious slap from a soldier ends the moment and causes Jesus' lips to bleed. The trickle blends with the blood streaming from the spiny thorns slicing into his scalp and ears. Joe loses sight of him because as many that can get near him punch him or hawk phlegm on him. The executioners pick him up off the ground and heave the wood upon him; making him carry the cross that will torture him to death is a humiliating touch. The splintered wood carves his shoulder. He can barely stand. He hasn't eaten or slept. Somehow, he keeps going.

The people bellowing for his death are some of the same folks who, a week before, triumphantly welcomed him as their king. Now they will not stop screaming at him. Joe thinks about screaming with them.

Louder and louder and lewder. Raise the sound and lift it, unleash the cries!

Crucify him! To his surprise, Joe says it too, but just once and softly.

Jesus says nothing.

The crowd follows Jesus with a festive revelry. Most do not understand or care about the complex religious, cultural and political factors involved. An execution was something to do, a spectacle breaking up the daily routine. Joe moves along with the crowd, a pebble now circulating in his hand. Jesus moves slowly down the dusty streets, collapsing several times. Each step is an absolute decision, especially when sweet relief is always within his grasp. The cross is unfathomably heavy, laden with all sins. Each step is an act of obedience.

Crucify him!

With vile language they antagonize him but Jesus remains quiet. And somehow, for some impossible reason, he keeps going.

Joe screams "Crucify him!" Everyone else is doing it.

The lively execution party reaches the hill of Cavalry, just outside the city. Joe watches as the soldiers attach a sign to the top of the cross. It reads INRI. The letters stand for "Iesvs Nazarenvs Rex Ivdeaorvm."

Jesus of Nazareth, King of the Jews!

This is the final insult. Where was the great and eternal kingdom he so often spoke of? All the onlookers and those passing through the big city will read the sign and know that this is what happens when you try to disrupt the way things are around here.

The soldiers strip him naked and arrange him on the wood. Joe cheers with the others. Jesus finally speaks as they pound iron spikes through his hands – but only to beg forgiveness for them. A nail rips through his feet, bringing flesh with it out through the back of the cross. He gasps when the nails penetrate him. Joe does too. Jesus' eyes close and his mouth tightens as the body tries to circulate adrenaline to relieve the trauma. In a moment, it wears off and he knows nothing but suffering.

Now the cross is lifted high into the still desert air and the agony is so pronounced that the people stop cheering. A makeshift crown of thorns obscures his trampled face. He can't lean his head back because that lodges the thorns deeper into his skull; the muscles of the neck burn and crave relief but there is none.

The mood shifts. His enemies try to stir the crowd again but even they can't bear to watch. The folks who came for a spectacle are instead aghast at the sight of this person choking to death.

Crucify him?

Crucifixion is the zenith of suffering, the most horrific manner of execution ever devised. It is so sickening and unsettling that upstanding Roman citizens were not to speak of it much less watch it. Slowly – that was the key to it. Death comes from asphyxiation. The condemned continually needs to push down on the nail through his feet to hoist himself up and clear the rib cage to draw a breath. Gravity pulls the chest downward but the nails through the hands keep the torso up. So he starts to suffocate. Then he must choose between the unmitigated agony of trying to stand up on a spike going through both feet and the brutal terror of asphyxiation. Unrelenting, cyclical agony. A few seconds later he must choose again. It is a wheezing, gasping death. Torture. Slow.

Jesus tries to stand but his knees give out and his body falls only to be caught by his hands tearing against the spikes.

The word 'excruciating' means "from the cross."

In the bedroom, Joe yawns again. His knees hurt from kneeling. Some part of him registered all the other things he could be doing and lamented that he wasn't even halfway through this meditation. He thought of ice cream. His guardian gently reminded him where he left off.

The young man's death takes several unbearable hours. The name of the place on whose outskirts the execution occurs means "City of Peace."

Those onlookers who have remained squirm because it is taking so long. They wished he would just die already. But those who have the stomach to remain are also the most audacious and their words slice him.

"If you are the Messiah, come down from that cross!"

"Didn't you say you could build up the Temple in three days? Not so tough now."

"No miracles today, eh, Teacher?"

Joe thinks about intervening, saying something, doing something, but he doesn't want to stand out. He feels powerless to help so he yells a few things, but nothing really, really mean.

The crucified man's few friends have not only abandoned him, they denied ever knowing him. The afternoon sun is unforgiving. Jesus is parched. Through the blood-drenched hair in his eyes, he sees a familiar face. All morning and afternoon, his mother has watched her son being slaughtered. She is in front of the first row of onlookers, only a few feet from the cross. She would never leave him; she is dying along with him.

Has it been 10 minutes yet?

Mary turns to look at Joe. Even at a distance, he has never experienced such tenderness. Her eyes invite him to approach the cross. He can't look at her and he prefers the safety of the crowd.

The soldiers laugh and drink while Jesus chokes to death. There is spittle and the mutterings of an old Psalm on his cracked lips. Those performing the execution roll dice to see who gets his garment, the dying king's only possession. Shredded nerve endings grate against the iron piercing his flesh. He tries again to stand for breath. Death is the only hope now. His death is their only hope.

His little movement of love is vanquished under a savage outpouring of violence. What crime did he commit, this loneliest criminal? He is a man most gentle, utterly kind. Weren't the only adjectives he ever used to describe himself "meek" and "humble?" Didn't he care for everyone who implored his help, with no conditions or exceptions?

His popularity made the religious authorities nervous. The crowds loved him because of the way he loved them. He taught them and laughed with them and provided for them. He healed them of everything. Here was a Messiah who was dirt poor and kept company with the outcasts of society. The ruling elite had envisioned a Messiah enthroned in splendor who would raise up a devastating army to obliterate Israel's enemies. Not this itinerant preacher and his bumbling band of misfit followers. Why couldn't he be a warlord Messiah riding a golden chariot? That would have made him easier to accept - and understand.

Instead he preached love, but not easy love. There was no convenience in the selflessness he demanded from those who would follow him. In fact, the more difficult it is to love someone the more specifically he requires it. His commands were difficult, impossible:

Be perfect.

Sell everything.

Love your enemies.

Hate your life.

Eat my flesh.

Drink my blood.

Take up your cross...

And where was this kingdom he always talked about? What king has no army, no power, no wealth? What kind of king called himself the servant of his friends? What kind of king honored women, refused to objectify them and elevated them to equality? What kind of king touched lepers and dined with beggars? What kind of king was born in a barn? Who says to eat their flesh and drink their blood? Who, indeed, but this man?

But all that was over now. The establishment had crushed him. This crucifixion would serve as a warning to all his followers and the next self-proclaimed Messiah. In a few weeks, no one would remember his name. Order would be restored.

The crowd continues to dwindle. The show is mostly over.

His breathing slows. Precious blood trickles from a litany of gashes and wounds. He has no strength left. What kind of king dies this way?

His chin moves. He is about to say something. Everyone hushes. He lifts his head and squints against the sunshine. He speaks but his voice is loud – how? There is hardly any life in him but he reaches back, down past the horror of the sins he is carrying and into that still temple where each person is defined. He summons a single statement, his last will and testament. One last thunderous burst of breath and life. His voice is powerful and he speaks with absolute authority.

"It is finished."

The work he was sent to do by Another on behalf of many others is accomplished. The coronation of the King is complete.

The sky's blue blackens into a midday night. Death does not take him, it can't take him. He gives himself voluntarily.

Then God bowed his head and he died.

23

Joe wiped tears from his eyes. It was difficult to comprehend that something so ugly was perpetrated against one so beautiful. And what was this new thing during tonight's meditation? *Why was I taunting you? Why did I go along with them? I would have been on your side, right? And what does this mean for all the stuff that's happening?* Joe got up and eased into his bed. His circumstances had not changed nor did he have any new answers but he experienced peace inside. He asked the Holy Spirit to help him understand it all.

He pulled the covers over himself and flicked off the bedside light. Sometimes Angela liked to paint at night and came to bed later. An insight came to him like a spark glinting inside a dirty glass. *So, Jesus did not* deserve *what happened to him. I don't* deserve *all the stuff that's happening to me, either, but neither did I* deserve *everything I enjoyed before all this.*

He thought of the apostles, Jesus' hand-picked companions. *They spent every day with him for three years. They ate with him and walked with him. They saw all the miracles firsthand. And when it was go-time they all scattered. I tell myself I would have done better than they did but don't I do the same thing? I claim to follow him but then there's something I know is wrong and I do it anyway.*

Joe B. told the Lord God he wanted to unite his suffering to the suffering of Jesus on the cross. He thought about the way Jesus looked at him through the crowd. Even in the midst of so much violence, he was entirely gentle and compassionate.

His prayer continued this way for a long time - free form, formless.

I have no idea why these things are happening to me, but I know you do. It feels like my life is unraveling, Lord.

Please, help me to trust that you have a plan for all of this. I'm sorry for all the times I've abandoned you. Thank you for never abandoning me.

He prayed this way until sleep overtook him. He closed his eyes and then his dreams became a prayer.

104

24

Tori Rowan Making Rounds on Late-Night Talk Shows; Modeling, TV Deals Up Next?

By Millie Keefe
Daily Sentinel reporter

Tori Rowan, Hollywood's newest darling, continues to see her star skyrocket in the wake of her sexual harassment lawsuit against her former employer, Joe Brescia. The 30-year-old stunner has appeared on several late-night talk shows this week to discuss her upcoming book.

The book is only the beginning of what promises to be a lucrative journey for the former paralegal. Rowan has already signed a long-term representation deal with the prestigious Winston Talent Group. She refuses to discuss the specifics of her lawsuit but readily chats about her media plans.

"It's just a blessing," the Long Island native remarks. "A few weeks ago, I was in a living hell and now I have all this going for me. It's true: good really does come out of evil. I am so excited to take the next step. I have a few endorsement deals in place but I'm most eager to start working with women who have undergone similar experiences."

COMMENTS SECTION|YOU MUST BE A REGISTERED USER TO COMMENT, ALL COMMENTS ARE SUBJECT TO THE DAILY SENTINEL SUBMISSION GUIDELINES

DebbieVizz: Jesus is the answer

Donnamass: She is so pretty! I love how hair is always perfect xoxoxox

Stink3: I made hundreds of dollars answering a few simple questions! Click this link to cash in today!

MidGardEn: How was she not discovered b4 this? Damnnnnnnnnnnnn

Tonight.Tonight: Tori if ur reading this I love you!

Staggeredconformity: who is she dating?

JuJuMiLa: American Dream

Doogie: no wonder he harassed her...goodness grashee

GiadaLuciano: I don't think it's rightg that she is cashing in on all this. They haven't even gone to court yet. Seems funny to me

NEXT | PAGE 1 OF 307| LAST

25

SATURDAY, APRIL 15

Juliana was the first to finish packing - she always packed the fastest. She ran to her mother and hugged her and her brother in the womb. Valerie and Michael had tried for years to get pregnant again after Juliana was born. The baby would come next month. They hadn't told anyone yet but Michael and Val had decided to name the boy after Joe.

"I'm all done, Mommy. Are we almost ready to leave?"

Val stroked Juliana's black hair. "Just about. Daddy ran out to get a new cooler. We'll leave when he gets back."

Juliana brought the luggage out to the driveway, near where her father would park. Val sat on the front steps while Juliana performed her martial arts routine on the grass. The precision devolved into a routine of cartwheels and singing and silliness. After a while, the girl came back to the porch and curled up on her mother. They remained quiet this way for a while.

A postcard-worthy spring afternoon played out in their leafy Westchester neighborhood. The sky was painter's blue and decorated with perfect, puffy clouds spilled from the inside of some heavenly pillow. A slight breeze stirred the leaves, which squirmed before resettling in line on the branches.

It was a beautiful day for a drive.

"Daddy's back! Time to go!" Juliana trilled as her father's black Lexus came down the street. She helped her mother get up. Michael parked and began loading the bags in the trunk.

"We're going for two days! You guys packed for a world tour," he called out over the lawn.

Michael put the new cooler next to the bags and closed the trunk. He walked up the little path to the front porch and kissed his wife on the lips.

"Oh, your dad called. They don't need a ride. He got held up with his attorneys..." Val spoke discretely because they had not yet informed Juliana about the accusations aimed at her grandfather. Michael and Val knew that she would be crushed.

"He said that they would meet us in New Haven. He and your mom are going to take the train from Grand Central this afternoon. We just have to pick them up at the train station later."

"Poppy and Grandma aren't coming with us?" Juliana was disappointed. She was looking forward to playing games with Joe in the backseat.

"I guess not, Jules," her father said, shooing a bee away from his daughter's ear. "You can take a ride with me to pick them up later if you want."

"Alright. Ready Dad?"

They helped Val ease into the front seat and they departed for New Haven. The drive would take about an hour and a half. The little, growing family prayed together as the car pulled out of the driveway.

In the name of the Father, and of the Son, and of the Holy Spirit...

26

Bruno Sangri awoke late that morning, sweating, with a new thought grinding into his consciousness.

Find them. His raspy breathing seemed to sync with it. *Find,* he breathed in. *Them,* he breathed out.

He struggled to get out of bed. A delinquent payment notice had been slid under the front door. Though formal, it had a handwritten note attached to it. It was from his landlady.

Bruno,

Are you OK? I tried calling a few times. It is not like you to not pay rent. We can work something out – just call me or come see me.

Dottie

He crumpled it up. Bruno stumbled to the kitchen sink and moved aside the dishes and silverware which had piled over the edge. He tossed the note into the sink. Bruno bent to put his cracked lips under the flow of water. *Find them.* He stood up and the cough returned, rattling inside his chest. It was so violent and persistent that he doubled over and steadied himself on the countertop. The cough produced blood which he spit onto his kitchen floor.

He found the handle of whiskey from the night before and drank. Bruno stood at the window, the bright brilliance of the late morning flooding through the deepening green of the trees. Strands of golden sunlight sliced through each branch and leaf. He could have cried as he stood there, either from the exquisite perfection of the natural order unfolding before him or from the misery that ceaselessly reminded him that his fiancée and his best friend were living together a few states over. He hoisted the bottle again.

Find them, Bruno. Go now. The notion burrowed itself deeper, pulsing seductively to the rhythm of his migraine.

Bruno found his keys and left the apartment wearing the black shorts and white t-shirt he had slept in.

It was a beautiful day for a drive.

Valerie was dozing in the front seat, two hands on her belly. Juliana started a book but didn't really feel like focusing on it. She plopped it onto the seat next to her and pressed her face against the glass to watch the road unfurl beside her. She catalogued the list of names she liked for her baby brother. The glass reminded her of her grandfather's office. She sighed.

Her father turned off the radio and slowed the car just before the highway on-ramp. Michael rolled down the window. He waved over a homeless person holding a sign. The man came over to the car. "Morning, Ron."

"Morning, Mike." They chatted for a moment. Juliana could see a few bills pass between them as they shook hands. Michael accelerated onto the Merritt Parkway headed north.

"That was nice what you did, Daddy."

He looked at her in the rearview mirror and smiled.

Bruno belched as he exited the store. He tried to get the key into the door. Several attempts later he was successful and fell into his car. Bruno tossed an empty can onto the seat next to him. It rattled around and fell to the floor near the empty whiskey bottle. He had stopped to get a six-pack for the ride.

Today was the day. He would go to New Jersey and pay them a visit. Just see how they were doing together. He noticed a screwdriver in the back seat, picked it up and placed it on the seat beside him.

He steered his SUV onto the Merritt Parkway headed south.

Juliana started to doze as they passed through Fairfield. The beautiful, sunny day and the pleasant whir of the drive contributed to her sleepiness. She closed her eyes for a moment. They were almost there.

Bruno began coughing as he drove past the exit for Fairfield. Mucus, phlegm, blood and spittle escaped his mouth and landed on the steering wheel and dashboard.

He felt faint. The perfect sunshine in his eyes and the clouds marching on horizonward, falling into orderly rows like seedbeds in a field. The road unraveling before him at ninety miles an hour.

The cough quieted for a moment and he took a desperate breath. He experienced an instant of peace. Then the cough returned, harsher than ever before, and shook him savagely. Like the devil himself was trying to escape the confines of Bruno's body. The cough rocked him and jerked him. His arm got caught in the steering wheel. The car swerved sharply and flipped over a gap in the median. It lost traction on an embankment and tumbled onto the other side of the parkway. Bruno's guardian angel pronounced the final blessing over him.

Michael saw it happen in slow motion. An SUV in the southbound side of the highway suddenly flipped the barrier and was hurtling towards them. His heart sank as the reality of the situation occurred to him. Michael thought of his family: his wife, daughter and unborn son. There was no time. His guardian angel steadied his spirit for the last time. The guardian had dreaded this moment but raised his hands to pronounce the blessing. Michael braced for impact and slammed two feet on the brakes. He opened his mouth to scream.

Satan angled himself to get a better view.

Juliana opened her eyes from her lazy little nap. She had no time to be afraid. She saw the SUV but couldn't process it. Her guardian angel whispered to her that everything would be alright. The last thing Juliana saw was the other driver's face. He looked so sad.

Sparks and flames exploded like fireworks celebrating the massacre. Blood and glass. The devil cheered the carnage like he was at a spectator sport. Rescue crews arrived promptly but there was only one person to rescue.

And the people stuck in the traffic caused by the wreck complained about being late and how hot it was.

27

Joe was in the shower when the doorbell rang. Angela peeked through the hole. A uniformed state trooper. She opened the door briskly.

"Hello, officer?"

"Mrs. Brescia?" He was young, handsome, solemn.

"Yes?"

"May I come in? And is your husband at home?" Behind him: another trooper, two women and a priest. A slender priest. Angela's hand began to twitch.

"Yes. What is it?"

"Ma'am..." his voice trailed off. "Is your husband here as well?"

"Officer, tell me now."

Then with courage – *just get it over with* – he delivered the message. "Ma'am, I am Sergeant Steven Kent with the Connecticut State Police. I am afraid I have some awful news to tell you. There has been an accident and..."

Angela's spirit plunged.

"...and your son Michael, your daughter-in-law Valerie were killed...and your granddaughter Juliana is in critical condition...I am so sorry."

No. She dropped to her knees, doubled over on the little table by the door. She struggled for breath. The trooper reached out to steady her.

She heard his words but rejected them. *This cannot be. Can not.*

"No...no, there must be some mistake. No, please, no."

"Ma'am...Mrs. Brescia. There is no mistake. I am truly sorry. We have some counseling people here. Is your husband here?"

The grief poured over her, poured into her, poured through her. Owned her. She dry-heaved violently and a moment later she vomited on the floor.

"Joe!!! Joe!!!"

He burst out of the bathroom tucking a towel around his waist. His wife was half kneeling, half clutching the dresser. A policeman supporting her? Other people standing in the doorway? Father Jack? Angela sobbed uncontrollably into the crook of his elbow.

Jesus, have mercy.

Joe was at her side in an instant. He crouched down next to her and put his face directly in front of hers, grabbing hold of her face with both hands. Water from his hair and towel puddled beneath them.

"What is it? Ang, what's wrong?" Angela's sobs became so violent that she lost consciousness.

"For the love of God!" Joe screamed. "Angela!"

He cradled her head in his lap. He looked up at the young cop, desperate.

"What the fuck is happening? Tell me! Tell me!"

"Mr. Brescia," the young man ached at having to repeat this message. "I am Sergeant Steven Kent with the Connecticut State Police..."

28

Joe moved in a dreamlike trance through the hospital. Numb and unable to communicate, he collided with people and things as he lumbered past. He looked and moved like a man disturbed.

A team of police and medical people, all whispering with dutiful solemnity, moved behind, alongside and ahead of him. They vaguely guided Joe to her room.

They approached the door and the people parted. Joe exploded into the room.

Juliana looked at him and then she died. She breathed for the last time, her gashed face composing itself and then resting and then stopping. Though violent, death covered her gently like a wave washes over the sand, as if in deference to her innocence.

She was immediately conscious of the grandeur of Heaven. She marveled at every prayer she had ever said and every prayer ever said for her, strung up like a trail of lights. Like lamps illuminating a path. The Mother of God, her guardian angel and the vast family of saints were assembled at the end of the path to welcome her home. Their smiles were so...*familiar*; like she had seen them before. They all motioned for her to turn around. Juliana turned and gazed directly into the face of God. She fell to her knees in bliss.

On earth, Joseph Brescia also fell to his knees.

29

City Prosecutor Michael Brescia, Family Killed by Drunk Driver

By Millie Keefe
Daily Sentinel reporter

Distinguished New York City prosecutor Michael Brescia, his wife Valerie and their daughter Juliana were killed Saturday by a drunk driver. The accident took place on the Merritt Parkway in Connecticut when their car collided with an SUV driven by Bruno Sangri, 35. Sangri was also pronounced dead on the scene.

Preliminary toxicology reports showed Sangri's blood-alcohol level was nearly three times the legal limit. Several empty bottles of alcohol were found in the wreckage of his vehicle.

Sangri's SUV had flipped the median and hurled into oncoming traffic at over 90 miles an hour, police say. No one else was injured.

Brescia was driving his family from their Westchester home to their beach house in New Haven, where Sangri was from.

Brescia had won several high-profile cases in recent years including verdicts against violent gangs and a child pornography ring. He was 38 years old.

Michael and Valerie were the son and daughter-in-law of Joseph Brescia, the former City Councilman and founder of the world's leading designer of airport x-ray equipment. The elder Brescia was suspended from his position by the board of directors this week after being accused of sexual harassment by an employee. He was also widely reviled when a malfunction of his company's technology nearly led to a terrorist attack.

City officials on both sides of the aisle were stunned by the sudden death of their colleague. Michael Brescia, a favorite of the mayor, was long thought to have a career in politics.

Valerie Brescia, a teacher in the city's school system, was pregnant with the couple's second child. She was 36. Juliana Brescia was 11.

COMMENTS SECTION|YOU MUST BE A REGISTERED USER TO COMMENT, ALL COMMENTS ARE SUBJECT TO THE DAILY SENTINEL SUBMISSION GUIDELINES

Commenting for this story has been disabled by the administrators.

30

Fluorescent bulbs at regular intervals diffused a sanitized light through the long corridor. Joe sat by himself in an empty waiting area. The light from the hallway did not come into this room.

Wet hands covered his face. Tears spilled through his fingers and wept down his wrists. He shuddered violently.

Joe had just identified the remains of his son and daughter-in-law and watched his granddaughter die. Many people, kind people, had tried to console him. Joe's voice was hoarse yet he screamed and screamed. Grief took ownership of him the way a tsunami does a sandcastle.

Angela lay in a bed on the fourth floor, checked in as a precaution after fainting. She was heavily sedated. Joe wondered if this was a dream. He would give anything for this to be a dream, even a nightmare. He promised to trade all his future dreams for nightmares if he could just wake from this one.

Joe drew a deep breath and closed his eyes. How often had he begun to pray in the same manner? As soon as his eyes closed, however, images of Juliana inundated his consciousness. His imagination betrayed him and amplified each gory detail. A surge of nausea erupted into wisps of saliva which hung from his mouth; he never thought to wipe them away.

Joe sensed he was going to hyperventilate. He allowed himself to collapse from the chair onto the floor. Face down, he screamed and thrashed. He pounded the floor with balled fists. He choked when his screams overlapped his sobs.

Manic, his mind faded and he lost consciousness.

Satan sat on a chair above Joe. He observed this poor creature, collapsed from exhaustion. He examined him carefully like a scientist testing a lab rat's reaction to various stimuli. The devil had been feeding Joe a steady stream of despair for hours, like an IV line dripping into his soul.

He had never enjoyed this much power over one person before. This was the closest he had ever been to Joe. From this vantage point, the devil could see the intricacies of Joe's soul and how the soul and the body were fused together. He saw the depth of intimacy with God and the growing ringlets of virtue. And the fresh scars.

Satan slid to join Joe on the floor and reached a hand toward his face. Joe's guardian angel, watching intensely from the other side of the room, lunged forward but stopped. The guardian snarled with a divine ferocity that made Satan recoil and withdraw his hand. The guardian, of course, respected the arrangement God had agreed to, but reminded the devil without words that the terms of the wager included "only do not lay a hand upon him." It was the most the guardian could do to help, like a chained sibling forced to watch his younger brother's torture.

Satan collected himself and realized the angel would not defend Joe. He smirked at the guardian. Joe's angel reached for his swords but then composed himself. The guardian did not know why God permitted this but he trusted.

Joe stirred slightly and the devil sat down next to him. The guardian prayed with arms and wings outstretched, his neck craned up to Heaven.

Like a delirious boxer after a vicious knockout, Joe tried to right himself. On all fours, in the dark room, Joe labored to pray.

"Father..." he sputtered the word and resumed his wails.

The rush of grief returned to rain blows on his consciousness. The devil had to capture Joe before he got too deep into prayer. Satan stooped over him and whispered into his ear.

Look what he has done to you. You deserve better than this, Joseph.

My Joseph...

Joe considered the thought. In the definitive moment of temptation, the devil leaned forward, wide-eyed, maniacal. On the other side of the room, the guardian prayed - his wings taut, his entire form pulsing. Satan offered the apple. Joe considered it.

Good. Satan encouraged more hesitation like this. The devil was trying to fan a single ember of doubt into an inferno of hate.

You deserve more, Joe. You know it. This is how God repays you after all your years of loyal service? Be done with him!

Joe's conscience panged and he collapsed to the floor, on his back.

Lord God, in this agony I cry out to you...I am destroyed...Hear me, please. I don't know what to say...My family...

The devil was incensed. He was running out of chances. Even wavering prayers are prayers. Satan knew if he were to capture Joe right now, he had to get him to stop praying. He had to turn Joe's focus away from God and toward his circumstances. The devil had one last tactic to use.

He guided Joe's thoughts to Juliana...her sweetness, her gentleness...then her bloody death. Her life extinguished. Her cold body in this very building. And how Joe would never be the same without her. He kept intensifying her memory. Her black hair, the happy moments sitting on his lap in his office, her crooked teeth, the way she hugged him. Her endless questions. Then: the explosive violence of her death.

She didn't die on impact. Maybe she suffered and cried out for you, Joe. She was dying there on the pavement, in the glass. Where were you, Poppy? Where was God when she needed him? Precious Juliana! Dead forever! The devil hissed these things directly into his ear.

Joe stopped praying. How could he love God right now? The urge to hate God curled around his heart. It was so inviting. For an instant, he not only wanted to doubt God but to curse him. He burned to trade a lifetime of piety for this instant of hatred.

Joe raised his eyes to Heaven. The devil raised his arms in triumph. The guardian opened his eyes.

"I trust you, God."

Satan jumped on his chest and straddled him, assailing him with every emotional anguish he could conjure. Grief seared Joe, branded him. The guardian resumed praying serenely despite the violence of the room.

Joe continued amid the throbbing sorrow. *The Lord has given me good things and now the Lord has taken them all away from me. Blessed be the name of the Lord!*

"Not my will but thy will be done," Joe muttered aloud. The two angels in the room, one fallen and one magnificent, looked at each other. The devil screeched a noise and then vanished. Face down and without beads, Joe began to whisper the rosary into the carpet on behalf of their souls.

31

Satan tried to project confidence as he entered the Throne Room. His soul, decayed and gnarled with eons of hate and sin, stood out in contrast to the dazzling purity that surrounded him. Satan knew he was going to be questioned. He was painfully aware that Joe B. had responded to the devastation levied upon him just about as well as a person could. The devil was unprepared for the inevitable cross-examination. What could he say to God?

Lucifer thought the angels would be furious with him for what he had done in Joe's life. As he entered the Throne Room, Satan puffed out his chest and put on a menacing scowl. The devil scanned the assembled Choirs of angels. He expected a Seraph to break from the ranks and challenge him with a flaming sword. *Where was Michael?* The Prince had to be around here somewhere. Not only did none of the angels come forward to challenge him, but none of them looked at him. The devil's hands unclenched.

The Most High God addressed Satan. As God spoke, the emotional tenor in the Throne Room changed from joyful serenity to collected focus. The angels formed a square around the devil. They stretched around Satan, enclosing him in layers and layers of legions. It was as if, since this conversation mattered to God, it now also mattered to them.

The devil felt so, so small.

God asked: "Where are you coming from?"

God's voice is simply perfect; the one who hears it wishes he would speak forever.

"From roaming the earth and patrolling it," he gave a true if generic answer and stared at the shimmering floor.

And the Lord said to Satan, "What do you have to say about my servant Joe Brescia? He has not abandoned his faith despite what I have permitted to happen to him."

A realization swept over Lucifer. It emerged from that part of the intellect which one often chooses to avoid, the dark memories which one does not return to: God allowed the devil a certain freedom to operate because God always transformed evil into good. The more a person trusted that God was sovereign during Satan's exploits, the more the affliction could be transformed into joy.

Satan knew humans could not fully understand this mystery of faith because he could barely consider it himself. Somehow, God was using the evil actions of Satan and his army of demons together with the mystery of human free will for his purposes, which are always good.

Satan felt like he was being used. Like all the torment and temptation he had produced over the millennia, while destructive, was somehow being channeled by God to *benefit* his human targets as much as their free will would allow. Competing thoughts swirled through the devil's mind. He was humiliated because he had been soundly defeated in his attempts to get Joe to forsake God. And he was livid that in Heaven he was hardly acknowledged by his peers. *Think.* There was always another out, always another excuse. He explained himself without words.

I wasn't given a fair opportunity. You protected his body and his health from me. The guardian didn't permit me the appropriate access, according to our agreement. I can take Joe with one more chance. How could you put such obviously unfair caveats on the wager? How could I be expected to have a legitimate chance at him when there were such comfortable boundaries in place to protect him?

The devil sensed an unspoken sentiment being shared by a few angels to his right. He remembered the nuances of their communication. They were remarking about the irony of him complaining about fairness and asking for second chances. Satan could not bear the embarrassment.

"Skin for skin!" he shouted. "All that a man has will he give for his life. But now put forth your hand and touch his bone and his flesh, and surely he will blaspheme you *to your face*."

And the Lord Most Just, calm and gentle, did not pause before saying to Satan, "He is in your power; only spare his life."

The devil emitted a grisly grunt, more relief than satisfaction. God had agreed again. He knew he had to make this opportunity count. His satisfaction was tempered by the new awareness that God was using all of his schemes for the good of those who love him.

Rows and rows and rows of angels parted, opening a narrow lane for the devil to depart the Throne Room. He was being dismissed. The walk out was unnerving because all the angels watched him intently but he refused to hurry up. Once clear of them, Satan vanished. He was eager to find Joe. His thoughts shifted from intellectual ponderings about the mystery of suffering and free will toward the carnal. He fantasized about the gruesome tortures he was now free to inflict on Joe Brescia. There was no need for planning or strategy now. It would be an all-out attack of unrelenting brutality.

"'Only spare his life.' That's what you said. You got it. Let's see how close we can come to the line between life and death without crossing it."

As he left Heaven, the devil wondered if the souls of Joe's recently deceased family members had watched their exchange.

32

TUESDAY, APRIL 18

Joe exited his car and stepped onto Wooster Street in downtown New Haven. He pulled up the collar of his trench coat because he didn't want to be seen, the sunny chill of a cold spring day notwithstanding.

He stood on the curb outside Messina's Funeral Home. The funeral parlor had been in this neighborhood for decades. He remembered accompanying his father here, to the wake of an *associate*, when he was young. Though New Haven was largely different from the city he knew as a boy – more developed and more urban – this neighborhood was unchanged.

It was dusk, or as close to dusk as it could be without being evening. Sparse clouds whispered in a sparse sky. The cold found its way in between Joe's leather gloves and the sleeve of his overcoat. It sprinted up his arm and died on his chest.

The parking lot behind the funeral home was just about empty. Joe couldn't remember attending a wake that didn't have a long line of people blotting tears, waiting to get in. He pulled a thin newspaper clipping from the inner pocket of his suit and verified the time and date.

Joe recoiled when he read the name on the obituary. He took a heavy breath, closed his eyes and steeled himself. Joe checked his watch. No sense waiting 20 minutes for it to start. He decided to take a walk around the old neighborhood until it began. He hadn't been around here in years. Joe justified the walk to himself but he knew that he was stalling.

Wooster Street was the spine of the neighborhood. It was known throughout the world for pizza but to Joe it was home. He grew up a few blocks from here, on the other side of Chapel Street.

Joe walked west. The windows of each home on this block told stories about its occupants, the way the eyes do for the soul. Crosses and crucifixes and Madonnas spoke to the deep Catholic identity of the neighborhood. Statues and icons of Padre Pio or Saint Francis emphasized the region of Italy from which each family hailed.

The bakery was still there. Garibaldi's. It seemed like the whole neighborhood would meet there on Sundays after Mass as wives picked up a loaf of Italian bread to go with dinner or something for dessert. Mr. Garibaldi used to sneak him a little éclair or put a few *sfogliatelles* in wax paper to take home to his parents. Down the block was the barbershop where his father never paid for haircuts. There was a little martini bar in between the two rival pizza places now. That had to be new, it used to be a deli back then.

On the other side of the city, in the Yale neighborhoods, colonials sprawled under yawning oaks and elms. Their grassy lawns contrasted with the brick and cement of Joe's block. Here, three-family homes alternated with squat apartments. No backyards. Here, blue collar families retained fierce loyalties to each other and their culture. In this neighborhood it was family above all else.

With each step, Joe's mind escaped the anguish of the present and sunk deeper into the comfort of the past. Each corner ignited a sensation, a kind of summary of memories. That sewer drain with the irregular piece of concrete. The rusted latch on the gate in front of the DeNicola's house. A brick billboard advertising a perfume sale that began in 1979 and hadn't ended. He walked through time and into a living journal of some of the firsts in his life.

First kiss: the alley between the laundry and the package store on the west side of Wooster Square. Sheila Moretti. He was walking her home from a Donn Trenner concert at the little club on Chestnut Street. It was the first date for both. They were 15 or 16. He wore his father's suit and it was too long and too stiff. As they passed by the alley, he was saying something meaningless. She pulled him into it and pressed her body into his.

First fight: corner of Franklin and Chapel. Salvatore DiMatteo gave him a bloody nose and a cut lip. Joe returned about the same. Joe told his parents that the fight started because Sal insulted Joe's mother and he was defending her honor but the truth was Joe accidentally stepped on his shoe inside the grocery store and Sal's friends jeered him into it. Neither of them really wanted to fight. He walked through the scene and imagined his 10-year-old self pinned under the older and heavier boy.

Joe came back down the other side of Olive Street and moved toward Warren Street. The backyard cut-through that he and his friends used to take while running through the neighborhood was still there. He remembered how to do it – suck in your belly and shimmy sideways between the fence and the garage. He performed the ritual again, a little slower and a little more carefully, but he made it through.

Stick-ball homers sailed through the fine violet sky.

Back on the street, he noticed the last names on the mailboxes. Some of the names were new, but not many. *DeNardis. Massella. Vizziello. Capone.* The names beckoned to him. Most of the stencil work had faded and the tape had long since peeled off but the names seemed to present themselves anyway. "Our family name means everything," his father once told him. "I would rather have my name than my health." Joe was on his own street now.

Maturo. Bednarczyk. Proto. Santora. Engengro.

Memories everywhere. The mailboxes called to him, inviting him into the past.

Valentino. Thurston. Arzamarski. Pepe.

His steps quickened. It was coming up. At the end of the next block.

Deeley. Egan. Mullan. Williams. Riedel.

He crossed the street. He was jogging now.

Linehan. Fludder. Demas. Capalbo. Pannell. Soderberg.

He stopped in front of it, huffing a bit as he caught his breath. The little house was a peach color now; it was white when he and Ang moved in. The shutters were rotted. Long grass clambered toward the windows. The disrepair stung him but it was still the house. Their first home, not more than a mile from where he was born.

He laughed when he thought about how small this place was. A tiny little palace with two tiny bedrooms and a tiny kitchen and a tiny couch and a tiny white birch tree in the tiny front yard. Their apartment in the city was twice the size of this whole property.

Brescia.

The name was barely visible on the mailbox but the outline of faint letters still pronounced it. Whoever owned the house now did not have their name on it. The mailbox was slightly ajar and Joe closed it for them.

He didn't care how he must have looked, standing on the sidewalk, staring at another person's house. This was still his. He and his new bride bought it from their elderly landlords and moved in. They danced in the kitchen. Sometimes they made love carefully and sometimes frantically. They had no money but some nights he brought home a bottle of champagne and they would celebrate for no reason at all. He remembered the way Angela looked at him while she raised the champagne to her lips. Her hair damp, skin glistening, her body lithe and coiling around his in the dark. Together, they experienced this life as it is: difficult and outrageously beautiful.

What a little family they were. When they were poor they subsisted on love. Sticky sweat in the summer and bundled blankets in the winter. They were rich in love, they lived on it; it was their currency and only income. Angela was a few weeks pregnant when they were married. No one knew. Then the baby came; he was so small that the wrong whisper could break him into a thousand pieces. His son grew up here, in this house, in that room right there. Joe used to scoop him up and throw him high in the air, the little boy's floppy bangs landing a second after he did.

When the boy was born, Joe burned with the solemn responsibility that makes young fathers want to be better men. He vowed to provide a good life for him. He would teach him to be a good and honorable man, the way his father had taught him. Joe vowed that his wife, the glory of his youth, would want for nothing. He got to work teaching others what the military had taught him and in time he made good on those vows. That was all a long time ago.

Michael. His son's name brought Joe rocketing back to the present, the memories disturbed like an unwelcome stone in a serene pond. Michael was the joy of Joe's life. They named him after Saint Michael the Archangel. The happy boy turned into a profound young man that cared about other people. What was it that Ang always used to say about their son? *As a parent, he makes it hard to be humble.* The young man had the enthusiasm of his father and the focus of his mother. He boldly and naively wanted to change the world, to help people, to ease their sufferings and punish those who hurt them.

And then the young man fell in love and his wife was kind like few are kind. Valerie. Simple. Tranquil. Graceful. Deeply, deeply beautiful. They were the most radiant couple Joe had ever seen. They brought light and beauty and peace into the world.

And then they had a daughter.

The wake. He looked at his watch. It was time.

Joe's head hung as he directed his feet back towards Wooster Street and Messina's Funeral Home. He was grateful for the memories earlier but now they did violence to him. The day around him was gone. It was dark now.

33

A police officer was now stationed outside the funeral home, her shoulders clenched against the chill. She recognized him. Joe nodded to her without smiling and walked inside, a new and hot anger already stirring.

Two employees greeted him politely and directed him to the first parlor on the left. They recognized him and looked at each other, brows arching quizzically. The funeral directors had anticipated some people attending this wake but not him. They expected protestors or activist groups – the reason they called the city for the police officer – but they did not expect Joe Brescia.

There was no one else in the foyer. Joe did not unbutton his coat or take off his scarf. Along the wall near the guest book, a freestanding black sign with changeable white letters tersely titled the occasion. The little sign was the only one here who could speak the name.

BRUNO SANGRI CALLING HOURS

Joe entered the parlor. A tan-colored light tinted the meagerly furnished room: it was only beige walls, simple chairs and the coffin. There was a woman sitting in the back row. She leaned forward, hands clasped, forearms on her knees.

Joe noticed the absence of flowers. Usually at these things there were gorgeous bouquets everywhere. The old-time gangsters used to compete with the size of the arrangements they sent. He also realized there were no photos or collages. No grieving family to decorate the room with mementos. Nor were there people consoling each other, whispering and rubbing someone's back. No friends telling stories. No one, at all. He had never been to a wake so bare. There was nothing here but the coffin and the woman and the tan light and Joe's furious anger. This was not a wake like any Joe had been to because wakes were about showing respect: there was no respect here.

The casket was closed. He looked away from it. A deep hatred swelled up into his throat. His jaw tightened and he breathed twice through his nose. As Joe approached the coffin, he felt like he would lose his balance because his heart was hammering in a new way - with violence and purpose.

He stood over the casket. It was a dull maroon, not the stately bronze he was used to seeing at memorial services for better men.

Cheap shit, he thought.

Joe's eyes were closed, his cheeks hot. He worked his jaw a little to restrain tears or words or both. Joe raised a fist to his temple and then put both gloved hands on the maroon coffin.

"I...I'm Joe Brescia," he started awkwardly. Then he didn't care how he sounded.

"I am Joseph Brescia," his voice had never growled like this before. Raspy. Menacing. "I am the one whose family you killed. I have some things I want to say to you."

He broke down.

"You could have hit a pole on that highway so that it was just you. I wish you did. But you hit my family. You killed my family. You stole them from me." Joe spoke softer now but his voice was still hard.

"You killed them. Michael. Valerie. Juliana. Do you know who they are? They are the good people. They brought good things to the world. What did you bring? You motherfucker. You don't bring anything, you take."

Joe put two hands on the casket's long metal handle.

He had played out this scene in different ways over the last few days, never settling on any course of action. He had seen the man's face on television before and the thought of it enraged him. Joe's grip on the metal bar tightened.

"You scumbag motherfucker. You took them. And I want you to know she was pregnant. My grandson. That's four of mine you got. *Vaffanculo!*" Joe dropped his fists on the casket, a thud plodding around the insipid room. Some tears settled on his leather gloves, others on the metallic bar or the dull maroon.

"Look at my life," Joe sobbed. "It's shit now. Like yours." He pounded the top of the casket once. It shifted on its bier.

The two funeral home employees came into the room, unaccustomed to such behavior in this place. The men called to him and approached the coffin. He ignored them. Joe grabbed the casket bar with an overhand grip and braced his back as if he were about to rip it off its support.

The employees intervened. One held onto Joe's shoulder, the other moved to stabilize the casket.

Joe whirled around. The glowing anger dispossessed his faculties. He snarled at the man holding his shoulder.

"Get your hands off of me. Do you know what he did to me?"

"Joe Brescia?" a woman's airy voice entreated with a lightness that was out of place among the heavy anger. Her voice was bright, vivid.

He turned to her, breathing hard.

"What?" It came out less harsh than he intended. She flowed toward him.

"Mr. Brescia, my name is Dottie Avino. Maybe you would like to have a seat with me?"

The funeral home employees slackened their grasp on his shoulders. Joe regarded her, chest still rising and falling. He was indignant that his great moment had been disturbed but also - curious.

He looked down when he felt her taking his hand. He didn't remember taking his hands off the bar. Joe let himself be led to the front row of seats. The employees looked at each other and exhaled while smoothing their rumpled suits. Deep breaths replaced tense gasps.

"What do you want?" he asked, sitting so that he couldn't see the casket.

"Nothing, really." She was around his age. Grayish curls. A thin sweater, buttoned in the front. Slacks. Sneakers. "What I *don't* want is for you to do something the media will talk about."

"Why do you care?" He had never sneered at someone so undisturbed.

"I feel awful about what's happened to you and I can't imagine what you're going through." Each time she spoke, her bright voice seemed to deprive him of some portion of his anger. He both resented her next word and desired to be intoxicated by it.

"Why are you here?"

Dottie sighed and looked around the room. "I was his landlady. I think I was the only person he talked to these last few months."

Joe studied her as she spoke. She was so plain but there was something about her, a distinct elegance of soul which many imagine they have and few possess. Joe instinctively sought to comfort her but caught himself and re-stiffened, resenting the momentary lapse in snarl. Yet, the more he sat with her, the more he desired to know about this woman's peace. There was nothing severe or stern about her. She was everything that was soft and melodic and clement. She was like two chairs rocking together on a porch on a summer night. She was the relief that washes over you when you realize it was only a dream. A door being held open for you when it's raining. The feeling when you pat your back pocket after you thought you lost your keys.

"I don't think you remember me but we went to high school around the same time. I was at Sacred Heart and you went to Notre Dame...I was a year or two older than you but..." she trailed off and smiled sweetly at the floor.

"But what?" he said, almost eagerly. He had known her for mere seconds but in the truest sense of the word, Joe enjoyed her.

"We danced together one time. The spring fling. You went with my friend Dolores Vollero and she was having a crying fit in the bathroom so you came up to me and grabbed my hand and..."

He smirked. "*Maggie May*. Rod Stewart. You thought it was a fast song and I thought it was a slow song. We couldn't get on the same page."

"You remember!"

Joe's lips curled up at the corners. "I do remember." They shared a grin and a moment.

"I've been so proud of you over the years. I told everyone about your company and all your projects. I got everyone at my church to donate to your Haiti mission after the earthquake." She paused and her tone dipped.

"I have been praying for you since...since everything started happening."

"Thank you. Yeah." he said, stiffly. Joe's demeanor hardened again.

He glanced down, saying nothing, eyes following her beads as they spun and swayed. She noticed.

"I have been offering the rosary for both you and him."

As he looked back up, his features transitioned from solemn to seething.

"What? Why do you pray for him?"

"For his soul, Joe."

"Fuck his soul."

She winced. "OK. I know. I mean, I don't know what you're going through or how you feel but I can understand why you would say that. And you know that our prayers could still help him. And if they don't, God will use them for someone else."

"Please. Seriously. You're wasting your time. You think this guy has a chance of going to Heaven? That's not a Heaven I want to be in."

She was all serenity. "I don't believe you, Joe. You know as well as I do that if, somehow, his soul is in Purgatory, then he will eventually get to Heaven." Dottie looked around the empty room. "And it's not like he'll have many people praying for him." Joe realized that she had paid for the wake.

They said nothing, both wishing the other would speak.

She did, eventually. "I would never tell you how to grieve. You have every right to your anger. I just think you know, deep down, that..."

"That what?"

"I'm just curious why you're here."

"I don't know. It doesn't matter."

"Someday," she exhaled melodiously, "someday you'll be able to forgive him. I don't know when. I'm not an expert at these things. I just think the anger is hurting you more than it's hurting him. I don't know. I think it's a process. Someday."

"Fuck him. Fuck you. I watched my granddaughter die."

He hated himself for saying that. She was only trying to help. He hated her for saying it though; for being right, for pointing to the reality when he only wanted the fantasy.

He realized she was holding his gloved hand again.

"You know, Bruno wasn't always..."

"Don't say that name."

She didn't object. "He wasn't always...a bad guy, the way he was at the end." Dottie looked up at Joe as if for permission to keep going. He said nothing but swallowed and granted it with his eyes and chin.

"I was in real estate for a long time. He rented a place from me in East Rock. Well, he and his fiancée did."

His eyebrows scrunched. "I didn't know he was engaged. Where is she now?" he gestured to include the empty room.

Dottie wavered, all of her a sweet sadness.

"She left him for his best friend a week before their wedding. His best man. He walked in on them together. He told me they *casually* got up and got dressed and walked out of the room past him. He never forgot how *casual* they were about it. Like it was no big deal. Like he wasn't even there. They moved to New Jersey together, I think. And he wasn't ever the same after that. They even had the stones to send him a card on his birthday. From the two of them. Like they enjoyed twisting the knife."

Joe didn't know what to do with this. She continued.

"I asked if he wanted to come to Mass with me. I was surprised when he said that he did. He came with me for a few weeks – he said, 'I literally have nothing to lose.' He actually started to look forward to it. We would talk about the Gospel afterward or the Eucharist. I felt like there was a slight change. I could feel it and I think he could to. I made an appointment for him to sit down with the priest. I had calls into therapists for him. He was open to it all. But something must have happened."

Dottie's hand came to her forehead and she squeezed her beads. He sat up in his chair, sad to see her saddened.

"He started drinking. He stopped going to work. He stopped functioning. And then he stopped talking to me. Even when he was really bad, really bad, he would talk to me. Sometimes he wouldn't say anything but he would just listen to me. Sometimes I would write him these little notes, ya know? To encourage him, to cheer him up. I never had kids. I guess he was like a son to me. It was good to look after someone. I cared for him, I did," she closed her eyes. Tears formed and then streamed.

"But he stopped caring. The booze... I couldn't reach him. He was a good kid. It didn't have to end this way." When the words stopped coming she looked up into Joe's face. Bright tears traced slopes down her cheek. Joe leaned over and embraced her and she let herself be embraced.

34

WEDNESDAY, APRIL 19

The next morning, as Joe's consciousness hovered in that space between slumber and awareness, his body sensed that it had been infiltrated and become rotten. In those last dreaming seconds, Joe's body became aware of the situation before his mind did.

His first conscious thought was of God; the next was remembering that his family was dead. It occurred to him that as long as he lived, each morning would have to be a choice.

Joe opened his mouth to say good morning to the Lord but his lips were obstructed from travelling their normal path by oblong, calcified boils. Pain streaked through his face and as consciousness replaced sleep, he became aware of the boils on his temples and cheeks.

With a pleading gasp, he touched the boils on his face with the boils lining the tips of his fingers. They were swollen and crusty. Joe blinked rapidly and he focused on his fingers; dozens of miniature boils competed for space along each one. They overlapped on his knuckles and in between each digit. The boils were misshapen, filled with pus. His eyesight moved from his fingers to his wrist, then to his forearm. Each stop of his vision confirmed the waking nightmare. His chest and thighs. On his shins and between his toes. He felt them in his scalp. On his manhood.

A surge of adrenaline erased the last vestiges of sleep as his brain interpreted his body's new form. He escaped his bed and yelped in pain when he stood because there were scores of boils on the soles and arches of his feet. He sprinted to the bathroom, waking Angela with the blur of commotion he left behind.

"What are you doing?" she asked blearily from the blankets.

Joe gaped at the creature before him in the bathroom mirror, aghast and unable to speak. His appearance, changed overnight, was revolting. His jaw trembled. Sweat streamed down his temples, dripping through whatever space it could travel between the boils on his face. He feared crying because the boils encircling his eyes partially obstructed his tear ducts.

Every boil on his body was inflamed and oozed milky pus which formed a putrid sheen on his skin. He became aware of the smell that pervaded his bathroom. The odor caused his face to contort as his nostrils sought fresh air.

Joe could not see an area of his flesh that was the same as when he went to bed last night. Guttural sounds emitted from his throat in lieu of words he could not form and thoughts he could not corral. He trembled.

"God..." The boils on his lips moved in unison with the word.

"What's the matter with you?" he heard his wife say despite the boils ringing the inside of his ears. The wave of adrenaline dissipated.

Angela propped herself up when he did not respond. From the bed, she could see Joe inspecting himself in the mirror. Was he shaving? Why wouldn't he answer?

Joe tracked the pattern of pain which occurred each time he moved. Each movement – every flicker and twitch – set off waves of stinging torment as the boils bent his skin in every direction. When his muscles writhed in reaction to the pain, that movement, in turn, ignited a new swell and a new cycle.

He felt violated, as if these were the fingerprints of some hideous fiend who had defiled him while he slept.

"What's that smell, Joe?"

Joe ignored the question. He screamed, partially to express terror and partially to test his vocal cords for boils.

Angela rushed into the bathroom. She caught sight of his face in the mirror first and then in front of her.

Her reaction was more disbelief than revulsion. It was as if she was confident she would wake soon and tell Joe about the scary dream she just had. For a moment, Angela took in the side of his face like she was observing a painting in a gallery.

He slowly turned from the mirror to his wife and she saw the reality.

"Joe?"

She recognized his form but not his features. Her eyes twitched and she dropped to the floor, unconscious.

Joe's body ignited in pain as he bent down to her. He pulled back; he didn't want to touch her because of the boils on his fingertips but also because he didn't want to infect her with whatever evil had permeated his life.

Joe Brescia did not know what to do. Angela breathed softly.

"Lord God...?" He looked over his skin and threw up.

This was his fifth day without Juliana, Michael and Val.

Joe leaned his back against the bathtub and slid down to the floor, grating and bursting the boils on his back in the process. Disoriented and hysterical, he sat on the floor among droplets of pus and wept. He was a monster and he was totally alone.

35

Dr. Daniel Ferrari stood and stretched. He had finally gotten Joe sedated. His personal physician could not look at him. Angela leaned against the bedroom door, holding a cup of coffee but largely ignoring it.

The doctor had never seen or heard of anything like this. Joe had his annual physical a few months prior and the doctor had pronounced him well. Dan was in awe of the physical anomaly he saw before him. What happened to Joe could only be an anomaly; the scope and suddenness of what he saw before him simply did not occur in nature. Dan wouldn't have believed it if he hadn't seen it for himself.

Boils were common enough, obviously. One or two hardly constituted an urgent medical emergency. When Angela called him, it was the panic in her voice and not the description of his state that caused him to leave the pre-med class he taught just before it began and rush to his friend's side.

Boils were not usually the concern of a person with his stature in the medical community. He had mentally catalogued what he knew about them on the ride over to their apartment, more of which he remembered from home remedies than medical school: *bacteria-based infection encircling the hair follicle...corn-sized protuberance on the skin...extremely painful...reddish and inflamed at first, then softer as they begin to drain.* He recalled an aunt telling him as a child: "Don't try to pop them!" *The oozing pus must be contained and the wound medicated...popping the boil spreads the bacteria over the skin. Usually treated at home and without drugs, except in severe cases.*

Severe cases.

This was the severest case *of anything* he had encountered as a doctor and the most gruesome condition he had seen in four decades of medicine. Few medical situations could cause nausea in him anymore; he had already vomited several times this morning.

He forced himself to look again at his friend, this time barely able to stomach the sight. There were *thousands* of boils on Joe's body. Dan could not imagine the agony. The doctor's lip twitched, trying to summon empathy despite his disgust. He turned to Angela and tried to put on a calm, authoritative disposition for her. "We will admit him to the hospital. This needs immediate...attention. I'll call ahead."

She nodded.

"How was he feeling recently – anything out of the ordinary?"

She shook her head.

"The sheets? The linens?"

"We slept in the same bed." Angela looked down at her own arms, smooth and healthy.

"Has he eaten anything unusual recently?"

"No, we hardly ate anything actually. Preparing for the funerals this weekend."

He realized her children and granddaughter had just died and the grief was still so raw. Was it possible that all of this devastation and humiliation had happened to them in the span of a few days?

Angela's eyes were wide and desperate.

"I am sorry, Ang. I was going to call and check on you guys while...everything was happening with the company. And, of course, my condolences. I was going to give you some time before I came to see you guys. Actually, I sent a card and flowers...you should have them tomorrow or the next day...I am so sorry Angela..."

He stopped stammering for the right words and just walked over to her. He embraced her, the tightness of the squeeze indicative of the fear they shared. She rested her head on her friend's shoulder. Tears moistened his blazer.

"What's happening, Dan? The things that are going on in Joe's life...it feels like he's cursed."

The doctor did not know how to answer a woman afflicted by such compounding catastrophes so he didn't. He learned many years ago that being totally present to a suffering person is more helpful than clichés or platitudes.

"Can you believe what has happened to us this week?" She pulled herself back and investigated his face, anxious for answers. "I don't think I can do this. How do I deal with this? What should I do? Dan, look at him. Why does he deserve this?"

Sobbing, she looked over at her unconscious husband. "Joe would do anything for anyone. He *does* everything for everyone. He prays all the time. He fasts. No one knows how good he really is except me. How does all of this possibly happen to someone like him? And all at once?"

Dr. Daniel Ferrari said nothing, encouraging her to continue.

"My son is dead for God's sake! Our family is fucking dead, Dan. What is the reason for this? Tell me. Please, anything."

The doctor looked at her with tears in his eyes, a grimace of sadness his only reply.

Angela closed her eyes, as if a decision or announcement were forthcoming. When she opened them, her gaze focused not on Joe's ravaged body but on the small crucifix adjacent to their bed. She wondered why God had abandoned them.

36

THURSDAY, MAY 17

Anchoring the living room of the beach house in New Haven was a big bay window. Juliana used to trace her fingers absentmindedly through its grooves. Joe reached a bandaged index finger to outline the whitish wood. Outside was the shore and the Atlantic Ocean and another gray day. He sat in a black loveseat under the window. She used to sit here, upside down, black hair spilling to the floor, feet crawling up the window. She would smile at him from this position, lips curling into a reverse frown.

Juliana's memory was splashed across this house like careless paint on a canvas. Her sneakers with the purple laces were still there in the mud room and a drawing of a telescope she made for him last summer was taped to the refrigerator. The little incisions in the pantry closet marked her growth throughout the years. The hardwood floor of the hallway which connected the den and the dining room was another memory: two months ago they had competed to see who could slide further in their socks. She won and gleefully enveloped him in a big hug.

Joe was surrounded by the many iterations of Juliana's laughing ghost.

Outside the window, a blustery day grumbled on. The sky was the color of metal left exposed for the winter - rusted, bleak, inhospitable. Ashen clouds choked the afternoon light. The sand was colorless, nothing like the deep, inviting gold that Juliana used to throw high in the air while constructing a castle on a perfect day. Joe took the blanket from the couch and slung it around his shoulders. It was the green and yellow family quilt that his great-grandmother stitched. He would have passed it down to her as the eldest grandchild.

Rain started to fall, amplifying the gray. He watched from the windowsill as the beach firmed then muddied under the downpour. The waves took on the shore begrudgingly, with only a perfunctory splash, as if they would rather not be at work on this most dismal day.

Joe caught a reflection of himself in the cold glass. He glimpsed the bandages and topical medications on his face, touched the sutures jagging across his forehead and cheeks. The surgeons had removed hundreds of boils from critical areas. The rest were being treated with steroids and medication. Whenever he moved or breathed, a ripple of electric agony discharged across his skin but in a strange way Joe was grateful for the boils. The constant misery they brought and the regular treatment they required provided some distraction from his grief.

Joe had refused any post-surgery painkillers. His wife and the doctors were baffled but he was adamant. He wouldn't answer when they asked why. His wife wouldn't understand anyway and he didn't care what the doctors thought. He knew that uniting one's suffering to Jesus' agony on the cross made suffering useful, powerful.

He still believed.

He and Angela had moved into the beach house. After the funerals. They had to do something, go somewhere, change something. It was her idea. Maybe this place would once again be the sanctuary they relished over the years.

From where he sat in the living room, Joe heard the refrigerator open. He stiffened. Ang had been keeping to the bedroom, he to the living room. She came in carrying a tray.

"Hey. Made you something."

Joe looked over the contents of the tray: toast and a can of ginger ale and his next dose of pills. "Toast. You made me toast."

"I thought you should have something in your system for the medicine."

"I really appreciate you sliding two pieces of bread into a toaster for me."

"What do you want?"

"Nothing. Not toast."

"I didn't know what to make. You haven't really eaten anything the last few days."

"I'm not hungry."

"Then what does it matter what I made you?"

"You're right, it doesn't matter."

"Look. I just tried to do a nice thing for you."

"So you eat it then."

She dropped the tray on the coffee table and left the room. The can of ginger ale tipped over and rolled toward the lip of the tray. Joe hated picking fights to keep her away but it was better than the revulsion on her face when she looked at him. Muffled sobs came from the bedroom. He reached for the soda and popped the tab. Joe took a little sip and turned back to the window and the waves.

At all times, his attention was divided between emotional grief and physical torment. They competed with each other, a two-headed monster, a hydra. Each head tried to claim him from the other. They never relented and they never rested; each desperate to prove it was the master of his shattered life. Joe now lived in the middle of their ceaseless combat, his life the collateral damage of their war.

In addition to the boils, Joe had become debilitated by throbbing migraines and earaches. They pulsed with vigorous malice and he sensed they were using his own heartbeat to synchronize their fury. The few times they didn't overlap were almost a relief. He had not slept in days.

The migraines and the earache were nothing compared to the other new torment. An unnatural thirst continuously occupied his mouth and throat. Joe had used the word "unholy" to describe it to Angela. Water slaked it temporarily but it always came back. It was the most severe of the plagues which thrashed his body and the least explainable.

Despite the gruesome collection of empirical evidence to the contrary, he had not recanted his belief that God existed and God was good. Joe could not explain why he clung to this last scrap of faith; that ability came from somewhere beyond him, just like his misery. His belief in God had become an old story he used to love to tell but now couldn't quite remember all the details. Joe was not and would never be the same but he remained fiercely protective of God's sovereignty. His wife believed the plethora of consecutive disasters had caused Joe to become deranged. His mutterings of scripture verses at the window reinforced the notion.

Their guardians did their best to promote peace in the beach house but arguments frequently flared up, fueled by their grief and the lack of answers. The sound of their disputes was interrupted only by the crash of the surf outside the window.

So a broken man suffered in silence, staring out into the gray as his soul dispatched wordless pleas into the sea and sky. He fantasized about the sweet relief of death. Joe tightened the big green and yellow quilt around his shoulders and looked out the big bay window, searching for answers and relief among the waves and the sand.

37

FRIDAY, MAY 18

Minutes and hours slithered by but sleep never came. Joe lay on the couch as gingerly as he could manage, watching the sun stretch and yawn and rise over the horizon. These few bright minutes were the only solace after a night spent pushing back against despair like an intruder on the other side of the door.

He was thinking of a fight he and Angela had at the beach house years ago. They were in the kitchen getting spaghetti and crab sauce ready for dinner and arguing over how to pay Michael's college tuition. She thought he should go to his dream school. Joe felt he should go to whatever school gave him the most scholarship money. She loved that boy and would do anything for him to be happy while he would be stuck with the bill. He snorted "You know, I hate your fucking sauce. I always have." He was livid, serious. *My sauce?!?!* She laughed so hard that tears streamed down her face. They told the story often over the years. Michael enrolled at his top choice.

Joe smiled sadly. *What I would do to have those problems again...*

It was about six when the sun crested over the ocean, light splashing off the waves and into his eyes. Angela would be up soon. He decided to try to broach the subject of God's place in their sufferings one more time. Joe was certain that she had lost her faith and today he would confront her about it.

The devil lounged behind Joe, his legs dangling over the armrest of the recliner. He managed Joe's symptoms like a maestro conducting a symphony of violence. He called for precise levels of pain like the conductor asking for more *vibrato* from the strings and Joe's body acquiesced. His body had become a grotesque laboratory for experimentation. Satan, as spirit, did not have to stop to eat or sleep so he used all his efforts at perfecting the pain. The devil had not left the living room in several days, nor did he permit any of his lieutenants here, to the extent that he was unaware of the status of any other operation.

Satan was Joe's constant companion now and he kept careful records on how Joe's prayer life had changed in the beach house. His prayers were more physical now; he offered God each grunt of suffering and each time he gritted his teeth to outlast a migraine. If he did speak a prayer, it was one of the Psalms. The Psalms were the most desperate.

Outside, the sun had risen. Joe put his hand on the coffee table and used it to prop himself up. He swung his legs onto the floor through crackling pain. The devil shifted the migraine to the frontal lobe and carefully increased its intensity. Joe clenched his teeth. Satan looked past Joe's skin and watched the machinations of his subject's anatomy react to the provocations. Satan was careful to respect the conditions of life and death which oversaw this wager. When he deployed an earache or a migraine, he looked into Joe's physiology to make sure no unexpected hemorrhage or aneurysm would take his life. A good torturer knows how to keep the subject alive.

Joe lifted a boil-blistered hand to his temple as the headache thrashed behind his eyes. He tried to stand up off the couch but the pain momentarily forced him back down. The devil lowered the surface temperature of Joe's skin and in a few seconds, he started to shiver. Satan discovered long ago that this unexplainable chill produced a distinctly spiritual suffering in his subjects.

Joe once again tried to stand up, this time getting to his feet with a groan. The sudden rush caused some dizziness, which the devil highlighted and exaggerated. Joe took a few steps towards the window to clear the little space between the couch and the coffee table. When he was in the wide part of the living room, Joe attempted to genuflect. In the last few days, Joe made it his solemn duty to try to genuflect every morning regardless of his body's condition. This was his most revered personal devotion to the Lord God. It reinforced Joe's now comically stubborn position on his life: *Thy will be done. Serviam.*

Joe's right knee reached the floor. He knelt for several moments, more trying to collect his breath than any act of extended piety. His guardian angel knelt beside him, placed his shoulder under Joe's arm and wrapped a wing around his waist. The guardian leaned into him and helped him rise. Joe managed to stand up. The devil thinned his lips.

Sunshine drenched the room in light.

"Good morning, Lord." Joe could muster no other prayer.

Joe set his body down again on the couch and exhaled. He sensed hives forming on his hands. He closed his eyes. Maybe if he were lucky, he thought, they would never open again.

But they did. And when they did, he caught sight of a ceramic coffee mug on top of the piano. He had looked in that general direction all night but must have been unable to see it in the darkness.

Now, as the light filled the room, the white mug came into view. Juliana made it for him years ago. It held a place of honor on the wall of accolades in his office. He didn't remember grabbing it when he hurriedly packed up his office the day Larry and the board banished him. Maybe Nan had put it in his bag so he would be encouraged when he unpacked it? Maybe Angela put it out for him? He was almost positive it had not been on the piano all night.

World's Best Poppy

Her childlike handwriting mocked him. It was like being alive was an ongoing testament to his inability to protect her from death. He should have saved her, somehow sacrificed himself so she could be here.

The inscription morphed in front of his weary eyes. It retained Juliana's handwriting:

You Killed Me

He blinked and tenderly rubbed his face. *I must be seeing things. No sleep.* The mug's cheerfulness was out of place here in his palace of ashes. The tears spilling down his cheek were actually a balm for the scars on his face.

He grunted with surprising heft in his voice.

These were not his normal tears, though. The normal tears came because Juliana would never graduate college or walk down the aisle with Michael, maybe turning to wink at Joe as she ascended the steps of the altar. These were different. Tears of rage. A furious anger which demanded expression. It overwrote his weakness. Juliana had been *taken* from him *violently. Stolen.* Someone must answer for this. Blood for blood.

He stood up from the couch with more strength than he knew he had.

"Juliana!" The green and yellow blanket fell to the floor.

Satan straightened up in the recliner to watch. Fascinated. He had not prompted Joe down this line of thinking; this was organic.

With two long strides, Joe ignored his body's frailty and bounded over to the piano. Joe grabbed the coffee mug and smashed it on the side of the baby grand. The sharp crack split the silent morning. Powdery pieces fluttered unceremoniously to the keys and to the floor.

Joe lifted the remnant to examine it. Surprisingly, the circular handle was still intact and it was attached to a jagged, serrated blade that now comprised the remainder of the mug. It was very much like a short knife with a handle.

Joe hadn't spoken Jesus' name in days – he had only thought it during his prayers – but now he screamed it while lifting the makeshift blade to his neck. It was not a curse but rather the beginning of the most desperate prayer of his life.

Upon hearing that name uttered with purpose, the devil frantically abandoned his position at the beach house and retreated to hell.

The shard felt good against his hot flesh. His concern that the blade would not be sharp enough was dispelled when he noticed a trickle of blood staining his white t-shirt. He had hardly pressed it against his throat - it was plenty sharp.

"Lord, what do you want from me?! Do you want me to die? Then just take me!"

Joe sobbed and bled for a long moment, holding himself hostage as a ransom to himself. He wept loudly and asked God to save him or at least kill him. Each time his throat quivered in response to his sobs, new slits of blood glistened around the blade's edge.

His left forearm tensed. He squeezed the handle of the shard so tightly that the scabs on his knuckles opened.

"Lord! Please!" Joe emptied his strength on those words. If Angela was not awakened by the sound of the mug smashing on the piano, she would be now.

Angela. A rush of grief overwhelmed him at the thought of her being left alone.

For better or for worse, for richer or for poorer, in sickness and in health.

Joe knew he would not do it. He let the jagged blade drop to his waist.

He continued to sob. Blood trickled from several symmetrical wounds on his throat. The tears running down his cheeks speckled some of the deep red on his throat into a washy maroon. Joe asked God for *anything.*

"Joe?"

He turned. Angela clutched her robe across her chest. She looked delirious, as if he woke her during a disjointed dream.

"Joe, what are you doing?" She noticed the blood-spattered shard.

He lifted the blade again and brought it up to his right shoulder. There were dozens of boils there; the surgeons had described this cluster as the "non-essentials." He arched his neck to see the area better.

"If they're not essential, that means we don't need them."

He flayed off a row of boils, the weapon cutting smoothly through his skin. Blood and pus spilt from his arm and collected on the floor around the love seat. Angela brought a hand up to cover her mouth. He carved himself deeply, bright red blood gathering across his arms and chest. The severed boils dropped to the floor.

Then Joe switched the knife to his right hand and brought it up to his left shoulder.

38

"You have to realize by now," she continued an hour later, "that your understanding of God is wrong." Angela smoked a cigarette greedily. She put it out after a few anxious drags, directly onto the kitchen table. They sat immediately across from each other. Joe had never seen his wife smoke before; she had hardly stopped smoking during this conversation. The smoke from her previous cigarettes hung over them in a stale cloud. Angela lit another and took a long drag.

Blood swelled under the improvised bandages on Joe's shoulders. She flinched, remembering his self-mutilation which initiated this conversation.

"Joe, we have to be realistic here. The facts, they're undisputable: you got accused of sexual harassment. Your reputation is shot. I believed you and I stood by you. The company's technology malfunctioned at LaGuardia and you get blamed. I stood by you. Larry sold you out. I stood by you."

A new emotion rose in Angela's voice.

"Then. Then...Our beautiful family was killed by that fucking scumbag. That drunk. That fuck." Angela stopped and massaged her eyes with her thumbs. Instinctively, he leaned over to console her but she pushed him back.

"No," she swiped at tears. "Let me finish. Have you noticed a pattern with all these things? Bang, bang, bang? All in a row? It's not a coincidence, Joe."

Angela stamped out the cigarette and picked up another.

"*Then*, on top of all that, I wake up one morning and my handsome husband is something out of a fucking horror movie. Suddenly you become ...*this*." She gestured at him.

"So we move in here to get out of the city and it gets even worse. You sit in that chair all day and night whispering God-knows-what to God-knows-who. We were good, Joe. But now you have to hear the truth. I blame you for all this. It may be happening to you but it's affecting me too. My life, Joe. You wanted to play saint with all the spirituality but somehow it backfired and you took me down with you."

Joe swallowed deeply, eyes searching hers.

"I don't blame you for wanting to kill yourself. If it was me, shit, I would have done it a long time ago. I give you credit, Joe. I do. Your faith is impressive and you stuck with your story for so long that I think you even started to believe it. But it's time to face the facts. The fact is that if there is a God, he is not like the one you genuflect to every morning or the one you talk to on the roof at all hours of the night. Can't you see that?"

She took a drag and exhaled it directly in front of her. Angela brought the cigarette up to her eye level. The paper encircling the tobacco burned back unhurriedly.

"Do you know what I do at night? I am thinking about this rationally. And I figured out this all has to revolve around something you're hiding."

"Joseph. I want to know what you did," her eyes moved from the cigarette and locked on to his. "I know you did something. Was it an affair? Did you fuck Tori Rowan? Do people just randomly touch your belt, Joe? Or did you kill an innocent person in combat and now it's coming back to haunt you? Is that why you do all those good things for people? To make up for it? Come on. Look around you. You are being *punished*. Is it fair? I don't know because you won't tell me what you did. But take a good look at your life right now and tell me you're innocent."

She softened a bit. "Bub, you have to open your eyes. We had a good ride with God for a while but it's painfully obvious that's all over. And despite all this, despite everything, I have decided I am going to stand by you. But listen to me, Joe, I can't support you if you still cling to this bullshit about 'thy will be done.' I won't. So you need to decide. You really do."

Angela put the cigarette out. She reached across the table and took hold of his bloody hands.

"Bub. Listen to me. This is it. Whatever you tell me right now I will believe you. Just tell me."

He stared at her, incredulous.

39

SATURDAY, MAY 19

New Haven's Union Station throbbed with people, with motion and movement, with directed activity. Walking briskly, hands raising phones to ears or faces, the throng moved in every direction at once. As often as the crowd dissipated it was refreshed by newcomers emerging from the parking garage. Steam escaped a coffee cup positioned atop a baby stroller, the owner of both frowning into her phone. A digital information board had replaced the old clack-clack-clack flip-tile one. It flashed updates and delays, bringing groans from a pocket of people waiting for the 7:52 to Grand Central. Bill Sturm was the only soul in the station who did not need to be anywhere other than exactly where he was: eased against the lobby's curved wooden benches, hands folded over his generous belly, eyes closed. He had arrived on time. His friends Zoe and Elliot were still en route.

Bill did not mind waiting. It was what he had done the most in recent years. Being retired, unmarried and terminally ill gave him lots of chances to wait. And think. Bill had come to love the silence. He was no longer angry about being the tumor – that phase had come and gone. And he wasn't waiting around all day for death to take him either, he just didn't believe that his diagnosis was a ticking clock spurring him to do lots of things – fun and exciting things! – to justify his remaining time. His life was his own and Bill wasn't the type to need approval from others. He didn't have a cell phone or a computer, he had a garden. He preferred to be alone and he had come to appreciate the difference between loneliness and solitude. So most of the time Bill could be found among his plants, hands clasped across his gut - observing, thinking, being.

As he waited for his friends, his thoughts returned to Joe and the reason for their trip to New Haven. Zoe had told him what she knew when she called last night. He had been sitting so quietly, observing a fat caterpillar lumbering across a leaf, that the sound of the phone ringing startled him. He couldn't remember the last time it rang. "Ha," he said to no one. "That'll be Zoe." She was the only person who called him. She had always been the ringleader of their group.

In the years following their stint in the Air Force, Bill, Zoe, Elliott and Joe had vacationed together every summer. Then every few years. Then only as life permitted. Elliott was the talker, Bill was the thinker, Zoe was the planner. Joe was Joe. The boys teased her about her enthusiasm for getting together but each privately treasured her commitment to their friendship.

"Hi Zo," he answered the phone.

"How did you know it was me?" she laughed. That same laugh throughout the years: like a delighted child. But he sensed something else in her voice.

"It's always you. Don't tell me you're planning another trip?" He pretended to be annoyed but he loved that she cared to check on him every now and then. She was the only one who knew about the tumor.

"No, Bill. It's not that."

He was immediately serious. "Is it E or Joe?"

"Joe."

"How bad is it?"

Her hesitation said what she did not.

"Listen, it's really bad. Ang called me. Shit."

"Zoe, tell me now."

"Mikey and Val and Julesy were killed by a drunk driver. Val was pregnant."

Bill did not speak.

She respected the moment he was experiencing. His breath came and went and came and went. After a full minute, she offered "I know you don't get too much news over there so I wanted to tell you."

He didn't believe in a higher power but all he could think was *God, no.*

"There's more."

"What?"

"Joe is in the hospital. He had some kind of incident. Ang wouldn't really describe it. She just said it's very bad. And that we should come right away. I just talked to E. We're going to take the train in the morning. Can you meet us at the New Haven train station tomorrow morning and we'll all go to Saint Raphael's together? I looked it up for you – there's a 7:20 you can take and we'll all get in around the same time."

"I'll be there."

They hung up a moment later and for the first time in many weeks Bill was neither still nor recollected. He leaned over his counter, unwilling to trust himself to stand on his own. He swore he could actually feel the tumor growing and squeezing tighter around his spine.

That night he dreamt of a fat caterpillar wriggling inside a transparent chrysalis, life-giving nutrients impelled and illuminated by golden sunshine. But it was not slowly transforming into a butterfly. In the dream, the pupa was methodically constricting around the caterpillar, contorting and suffocating the creature, its half-developed wings bulging and bursting as the sac tightened. The animal died inside a coffin masquerading as a womb while the indifferent sunshine roasted its remains so that they became foul and rotten.

40

SUNDAY, MAY 20

The only sound in the hospital room came from the monitoring equipment that the nurses had rigged up to Joe. Elliott, Zoe and Bill sat around his bed, waiting for him to wake up, lost in thought and various stages of fatigue. Bill noticed that the sounds came in three distinct types because Bill paid attention to things like that: there was the typical *deet* of the heart monitor, a flat *essss* from the inflation of the oxygen bag and the angry *cleep-cleep-cleep-cleep* when the IV needed to be refilled.

It was 9:09 pm. The last time anyone spoke, he remembered, was 6:09 pm. He knew that because Bill liked the little details. That was the time they had convinced Angela to go home and get some sleep. They had kept vigil since then. Sometimes dozing. Sometimes fidgeting. Sometimes looking at Joe. Sometimes looking at each other. Their silence was not like the silence between strangers on a bus. This silence was the kind which only people who trust each other can enter.

Bill looked over at Elliott – this had to be a record for the guy. E could not be silent for several minutes, much less several hours. Elliott wore a red flannel shirt, jeans and big brown boots, which Zoe had shooed off the edge of Joe's bed four times. He had hair that reached his shoulders, a tanned, outdoorsy face and something to say about everything. Where E went, silence retreated.

Bill and E had definitely dozed off. Bill glanced over at Zoe: she definitely had not. She was on the other side of Joe's bed, elbows bunching up the sheet, chin resting on her thumbs. She had been perched that way for quite a while although Bill failed to note the exact time. Zo looked like she was trying to cure Joe by sheer force of will. Her hair was pulled up in a messy bun, more streaks of gray crawling through the blonde pile than he remembered. She wore a white cotton tank top under a pink cardigan which she adjusted often. She had a hemp bracelet on one wrist and any number of bangles on the other.

Bill was thinking about the scratching sound the blood pressure cuffs made when Joe stirred. The sedatives were wearing off. Zoe called his nurse, Hilary, who came in to help him get oriented. He looked like he was going to fall back asleep when he registered the faces gathered around him. Joe laughed and shook his head, as if reprimanding himself for being surprised that they were here.

Elliott didn't wait to be asked. "Angela called us. Well, she called Zoe and you know Zo. Always has to be a group thing, right Zo? Yeah, umm, Ang said you hurt yourself at the beach house. You wouldn't stop bleeding and you passed out. She called the ambulance and they brought you here. They patched you up but you really did a number on yourself, buddy. You cut down to the muscle. With a piece of a coffee mug! What a badass! Lost a lot of blood too. What is that all about? So, like the nurse said, you have been in and out of it. The three of us got in this morning. We sent Ang home after dinner. Poor thing is exhausted. But we've been holding down the fort. Some cute nurses you got here, bud! A coffee mug, really? You were going to ice yourself over a few pimples? You got soft on us, buddy!

"Glad to see you too, E." Joe grimaced as he sat up. They all scooted closer because his voice was frail.

He took in Zoe. "Hi Zo."

She leaned forward and wrapped him in as much of a hug as the tubes and devices would permit. He hugged her forearm as best he could.

Joe grinned at Bill. "Pipe down Bill."

"Hi Joe."

"How long has it been?"

a few years."

"I know you know exactly how long it's been."

"We last saw each other on September 27 of last year when you and Ang made me come over for dinner. The last time the four of us were together was seven years ago."

A pause, not an unpleasant one, floated through the room.

"We wanted to be here with you buddy." This was Elliott.

"Thank you, guys." Joe reddened. "Means a lot. Bet you didn't think our next get-together would be like this."

Their eyes travelled over the tubes coming in and out of him and the bandages on each of his shoulders. They had heard him groan while he was asleep. Angela tried to explain about the earaches and the migraines and the thirst but they got lost or overwhelmed in medical details.

"Angela caught us up on everything with the girl and the lawsuit. And the company. And now this." Zoe dabbed at her eye. "And Joe we are so, so sorry about Mikey and Val and Jules."

A pause, now an unpleasant one, settled over them.

"We're here for you, buddy."

Joe examined the ceiling. Two or three times he started to say something but stilled himself. Then he began, desperately.

41

He paused to sniffle and wipe tears. "It might sound like a cliché, but it's true - I wish I had never been born." Joe was 11 minutes, according to Bill's count, into this assessment of his life. "I wish the doctor offered my mother condolences instead of congratulations. I would only tell this to you guys and Ang. I don't want to live. Look at me. I didn't kill myself but, man, I was this close. Being falsely accused, having the company taken from me, even this...this one-man plague I caught...they are *nothing* compared to how bad I miss them. I just miss them so much. I miss her." Zoe's hand shot forward, covering his.

Silence eased into then overtook the hospital room.

The *deets* sounded with more frequency. It looked like Joe was about to resume his discourse but lacked the strength. He slumped back into the pillows and scratched the stubble on his chin.

"What do you guys think about what's happening with me?"

Bill, Zoe and Elliott exchanged glances. E, typically, broke the ensuing silence.

"Well, bud. I've been thinking a lot about this situation. And you know I say this as a friend..."

"Say it, E." Joe's voice firmed.

"What did you do?"

Zoe interrupted. "Goddamnit, Elliott. We discussed this."

"No," Joe waved her off. "Finish."

Elliott was as solemn as they had ever seen him. "Look, man. I don't know much about religion but I believe that what goes around comes around. Karma. You've done lots of good for people, buddy. And you were rewarded for it. You had...well, everything. And now...yeah. It fits the pattern, doesn't it? Karma. Is it possible you did something you can't quite remember? Because if you're innocent – *really* innocent – then God has a really fucked up way of paying you back."

"You think I did something to deserve this?" *Deet.*

"No, man. Well, maybe. Joe, this is some biblical-level shit going on here. You've just gone through more shit in a month than anyone could in ten lifetimes. I love you dude. I'm not here on some sort of investigation. But at some point you look at the extent of this and you have to say this is not random." He trailed off and then, carefully: "Is there anything you want to tell us?

Joe regarded him then shook his head.

"I would tell you guys if I had done something, something big like you're suggesting. Of course, I've done things wrong in my life but I don't have some great secret crime. Ang thought the same thing."

Deet. Deet.

His voice picked up some snarl. "I beg you to show me what I did. Because at least then there would be a reason."

"Why doesn't anybody believe me?" The lines on the heart monitor squiggled and the *deets* pinged enough that the nurse came to check on Joe.

Zoe was incensed by what E had said but not surprised. Elliott said hard things to people if he believed they needed to hear it. She wouldn't be surprised if Joe dismissed them now. But instead, he turned to Bill.

"What do you think?"

"I can't explain why this is happening and I sure as hell don't know how to fix it. I would take it all away from you if I could but there's nothing I could say or do to help you. So I'm good just being here with you."

Joe nodded. "What about you, Zoe?"

"What, you mean, you didn't learn everything you need to know from Professor Elderedge's lecture?" She aimed a flat smile at Elliott.

"I don't know, Joe," she lifted an elbow and scratched the back of her neck. "I don't know if you're being punished. Maybe you're being...tested. Or prepared for something. Maybe you are being warned. hell, I have no idea. But I'm willing to jump in the shit with you and be with you as we figure it out. Or maybe we won't figure it out. But either way we will be in it together. That's all I got."

Bill's lower back ached from the uncomfortable chairs. He sensed the tumor there at the base of his spine, slowly subduing all the nerves below his waist. A spasm of pain ripped down his right leg. He tried to grit through it. Today was not about him, he didn't want to take the focus off Joe. He looked up to catch three pairs of eyes studying him.

"What's wrong, Bill?" Joe asked.

"Nothing."

Elliott: "You've been quiet, bud. Quieter'an usual, if that's even possible."

Bill and Zoe shared a glance which he tried to end but she did not permit it.

"You need to tell them," she was gentle but firm.

"I'm fine."

"Tell us what, Bill?"

"Now's the right time," Zoe insisted. "We're all together. God knows when the next time that will happen is." Elliott and Joe had troubled, expectant looks.

Bill considered this with his fingers clasped and interlocked around his gut. Elliott looked like he was about to shout at him.

"It's a tumor. Premalignant. Wrapped around the base of the spinal column. Cutting off everything below the waist. Nerves. Muscles. Hurts like hell. They think if they try to remove it I could become paralyzed. If it's cancerous, they say I'll have eight to ten months. So I'm kinda fucked either way."

"Holy shit, bud."

"Yeah, I'm sorry Bill."

Zoe said nothing but put a hand on his broad back.

Bill would have none of their sympathies, although privately he was relieved to tell them. He made a joke that since he and Joe were about to die then they needed to make this time together count. A few minutes later, they were telling old stories and teasing each other; every joke and tale a bit of ceremony, an oral pageantry intended to recall and ratify their friendship.

Another silence settled between them as the cackles stilled. Joe yawned and nodded at them. Joe could not remember the last time he had laughed. He fell asleep trying to figure it out. Zoe, Bill and Elliott waited a few more minutes. They picked up their belongings carefully and slipped out of the room.

Joe woke suddenly in the middle of the night. He tried to grab the tail end of a dream to stop it from fading, to examine it, to wrangle answers from it. But it slipped through the grasp of his consciousness. He sighed and offered the Lord God all his sufferings on behalf of Bill and the tumor and then was embraced by dreamless sleep.

42

MONDAY, MAY 21

Friends, family and colleagues had come and gone all morning. Mostly gone. Ang would meet the person at the door of his hospital room, her frame subtly but intentionally barring the way in. She graciously accepted their well-wishes and assured them that she would let Joe know they came by as soon as he was awake. Joe appreciated how many people cared enough to visit, but he had neither the strength nor the desire to answer the same questions or hear the same encouragement again and again. For those few she did permit into the room, she and Joe had worked up a system of nods to indicate when she would politely tell them *thanks so much for coming* and *he needs his rest.*

Joe and Ang had settled into an unspoken truce after the ordeal at the beach house. They had let the other speak their mind and that would have to be enough for now.

Nanette Romano was exempt from the head-nod dismissal protocol. She had been there all morning. Joe was sleeping. Nan showed Ang pictures of her dogs. Angela's phone vibrated and she leaned to the side to pull it out of her jeans.

"Zoe said they're on their way."

There was a knock on the door and a young man's voice asked if he could come in. A nose and chin tentatively entered the room. Angela jumped up, ready to resume her role as bouncer. Instead, when she saw who the nose and chin belonged to, she welcomed Eli Morgan with a big hug.

"Oh, Eli. He'll be so glad to see you." Nan came over and greeted him too. Eli saw that Joe was asleep and offered to come back later.

Angela huffed and ushered Eli into the room. Nan watched Eli take in Joe for the first time. Scars and scabs littered Joe's skin. Hundreds of lanced boils were covered in topical ointment. He recoiled momentarily before adopting a strong, caring expression.

"Seriously. You don't have to wake him up for me." Ang and Nan both started to insist that he stay when a voice from the bed said, "you don't have to wake me up at all." They all turned and saw Joe with as big a grin as he could muster. "I've gotten pretty good at fake sleeping."

Angela and Nan excused themselves to go for coffee. Eli sat down as Joe extended a bandaged hand.

"I'm not much to look at these days, huh kiddo?"

"Actually, you look about the same to me." Eli said with a wink.

"Funny guy over here."

"It's good to see you, Mr. B."

"It's good to see you, El. Thanks for coming."

"Yeah. Of course." He sighed. "I hate seeing you like this. I'm so sorry for all of it. Everything that's happened to you." They shared a long moment. Eli was afraid of the silence so he asked: "Does it hurt?"

Joe didn't know which aspect of his suffering Eli referred to so he answered for all of them. "Like hell. It hurts like hell."

"I wish there was something I could do."

"What - you mean you can't fix everything? What good are you? You're fired."

"Didn't know you could still fire people."

"You're right, I probably can't." Another pause passed between them. "There is one thing you can do for me." Eli nodded – *yes?*

"Tell me your thoughts. On my situation. On what's happening. What is your opinion?"

Eli's face scrunched.

"Come on. Humor me."

"You want me to tell you why I think all these bad things are happening in your life?"

"That's exactly what I want."

Eli had a faraway look. "I remember when you asked me 'how bad is it out there?' at work the day the lawsuit news came out. I didn't know what to say."

"But you answered honestly, which is all I want from you now. Look, the reason I ask you is because I have had lots of people – close people –all tell me the same thing. They told me how this is punishment for something I did wrong. Or I am being tested. Or purified. Or warned. Or all the above. Or there is no God and all of this is meaningless."

"I don't know, Mr. B. Not really a religious man."

"You don't have to be.

Eli studied his hands for so long that Joe was about to call his name.

"Do you believe in God?"

Joe paused. "Yes. I do."

"Well, then, with all due respect, if you know there's a God then it doesn't matter why this is happening. And it certainly doesn't matter what people have to say to you about it. If there is a God, and you are certain of that, then just, like, let him do his thing. I'm not saying it's easy. I have no idea what you're going through, Mr. B – or why. That sucks because we all want answers. I get that. You don't know what God is doing or why he's allowing this. Doesn't matter. What do *you* believe? And how are *you* going to live because of that belief? Do you believe God has caused this stuff to happen to you? No? Then he has permitted it. When people say God is 'all-powerful' I think what they really mean is 'God is powerful enough to make things happen the way I want.' I don't think it works like that. I think some of our struggles and sufferings do come from our decisions in life. Actions have consequences. Maybe there is a God, maybe not. Either way, I think you're asking the wrong question, Mr. B. The question is not 'why is this happening?' The question is 'is God who he says he is?' Now, I know it's easy for me to say all this when I'm not the one in your bed right now. But you asked, so that's my opinion."

43

Joe and Eli had been talking for the better part of an hour when Angela and Nanette returned.

"Hey guys. How you feeling, Joe?" Nanette asked.

"Never better," he faked a grin for them.

"Yeah, right. How's the patient, Eli? Eli will tell us the truth."

"I think he'll live. I don't know if he wants to, but I think he will."

Joe noticed that Ang hung back a bit. Actually, her cheeks were wet and red.

"What's going on?"

Nan put an arm around Ang and replied for both. "Joe, we ran into someone downstairs. You aren't the only ones who've been talking for an hour."

"Who?"

Dottie Avino poked her head in the room. Bruno's landlady.

"Hi, Joe." That distinct peacefulness accompanied her, like a shawl which she wore and wrapped around others when it was chilly. "I was on my way up here to see if I could pay you a visit when I saw Nan. We knew each other from church years ago. I didn't know she worked for you. She introduced me to your wife."

Dottie turned to Angela, who seemed to be both smiling and crying. "We talked a lot about what you and I talked about that night at the funeral home."

"Dottie told me about Bruno," Angela said to Joe, moving over to the bed.

"Yeah, me too."

"Sad life."

"Yeah."

"Maybe I should get going," Eli stood up.

"You don't have to."

"I know but I've hogged enough of your time. Thanks for the visit, Mr. B."

"Come back again."

He assured Joe that he would and said goodbye to the ladies. Dottie and Ang took the chairs on either side of his bed. Nan leaned against the window.

"Dottie has been telling me how he, how Bruno had a fiancée who left him. And how his life spiraled out of control after that."

Joe looked up at his wife, eyes probing hers, asking if they were really going to have this conversation now and here.

"She told me too, Ang. What about it?"

"Well, it's just that I realized something." She turned from him and faced the window, looking out over the skyline of downtown New Haven. The brightness streaming through the glass seemed to surround her, creating a two-tone effect where it seeped through her midnight hair. The light illuminated minute particles floating around her. Angela's index fingers wiped teardrops down either side of her nose.

"All these years, I didn't understand you, Joe. I didn't get what you were doing with all your devotions and prayers. But I think I just got a glimpse into what it all means. Talking to Dottie and hearing this kid's story, I just felt something come over me. Like a wave. It felt peaceful." She spoke to him but her gaze was now entirely fixed on the window, on the light. "I felt it for the first time since they died. It's not like I don't miss them, not like that. More like I was able to let the way I feel toward him down a notch." The stream of light entering the room through the window washed Angela in radiance, held her.

"I don't know what to say, Ang. I'm happy for you that you had that moment of peace. I don't think I'm there yet."

She moved closer to the window, captivated by the light.

"I know, bub. I know. I'm not telling you what to feel. Just that I think I get it now. When Dottie was explaining it to me - you know what I was thinking about? I remember one time we were driving back from Mass and you were talking about whatever the Gospel was that morning – surprise, surprise – and you said, 'That's the hardest thing about being a Christian.' And I think I said 'oh, what's that?' but I didn't look up from my phone. And you said 'Love your enemies. Bless those who persecute you. That's the hardest thing about being a Christian.' And I shrugged it off but now I think I understand what it means. It's really hard to do that, bub." The last few words were hushed under a wave of emotion.

Joe wanted to say something but the vision of his wife at the window, bathed in golden light, commanded his attention. Ang turned and faced him, sunlight flowing into the room, into her.

"I'm sorry, Joe, for everything." She started to apologize for specific things but he cut her off with an apology of his own. He sat up in the bed to receive her embrace. It was tight despite the sting in his shoulders. Nan and Dottie stood in the doorway, purses strapped on their shoulders. Despite some protests, the women said goodbye and left, closing the door behind them.

Daylight lit the room in celestial tones. Joe shifted over as much as he was able when his wife clambered into the bed alongside him. Sunshine enveloped them such that they felt its warmth on their hands and had to close their eyes against its lavishness. Her fingers requested his and she laid her head on his chest. They stayed that way for a long, long time; unhurried, wordless and resolved.

44

TUESDAY, MAY 22

Joe's guardian angel slowed to match his shuffle down the hospital corridor, accompanying him as he made his way to the chapel. He had managed to talk the nurses into letting him take a walk and get out of the room for a bit. Joe was weak but recovering. As they walked, the guardian greeted the angels of all the people they passed in the busy corridor.

Something was gnawing at him. Sure, he was relieved that Joe and Angela had a moment of reconciliation. That was beautiful; he and Angela's guardian stood back like proud parents as they accepted the grace which poured over them like light. Joe had not complained of the earache in two days and the medications seemed to alleviate most of the pain caused by the boils. And the fact that Angela had taken a step towards forgiving Bruno – this, too, was very good. But all was not well. An anxious sense tingled within the guardian with every hobbled step Joe took toward the chapel.

Satan. The guardian had not seen Satan in several days.

The chapel was a small space and the lights had been dimmed a bit to nurture silence. Joe blessed himself with the holy water and bent forward as much as he could as an act of genuflection. The guardian prostrated himself before the Blessed Sacrament. Joe eased himself into the first pew and his guardian angel sat beside him, his left wing curling around him. Joe prayed in a knowing murmur, the kind of tone reserved only for intimate companions.

"Hi Jesus, I'm feeling a lot better, thank you for that. And I am so grateful for that moment you had with Ang. You know I have been praying for something like that for so long, Lord. Thank you. It was inspiring to hear her talk about forgiving him this soon. That's honestly why I'm here, Lord. You and I both know my heart is not ready for that. But I've come here to tell you in person that I am willing to start the process. Or I'm willing to be willing. Or I would be interested in thinking about being willing to forgive him. Something like that. You know what I mean, Lord."

Joe cupped his mouth and yawned.

"I just sensed the peace she had after talking to Dottie. And I know it's still killing her inside. But it was there and I want that peace, too."

"I have to be honest with you, Lord. I have been thinking about what Eli said. And it makes sense to me. You are God and I am Joe. So, you don't owe me anything. But, Lord, these past few months...I don't understand why you would let all this happen. It's like you totally abandoned me. We had a really good thing going, you and me. We took care of a lot of people. I was really happy with the life you had given me. And you took it away for no reason. I just don't get it, Lord. My conscience is clear before you. I know that you know what's best so I am doubling down on my belief that you are God and you are who you say you are. But it's hard, Lord. I feel like it would be easier to forgive Bruno than to forgive you. That's just how I feel. Please answer me, God."

The guardian turned back to steel his gaze on Satan, who had taken a seat in the last pew. He was a nurse. The nurse's face was drawn, tight, blank. Resigned. Defeated. The devil stood and walked out of the chapel, mumbling about a plan for the next weapon.

Joe's whispered words ended and his spirit prayed for a while.

On the way out of the chapel, Joe stopped abruptly. The guardian scanned his thoughts and saw what he was about to do. He had expected this from Joe and was surprised it had taken him this long. Joe turned and hobbled quickly back to the foot of the altar. He knelt down as gingerly as he could. A rush of tears erupted from him, choking him in emotion. The feelings broke through him, a deluge of unexpressed desires, so that he nearly fell over before he had even said the first word.

"Juliana, my darling, I know you can hear me. Please pray for me. Please pray that I can find peace. I know it will take time. A long time. I have so many things I want to tell you. Oh, my little Miss. I miss you, Juliana, I miss you so much..."

45

SATURDAY, JUNE 11

Servers, white-gloved and black-jacketed, moved around the hotel ballroom offering a deferential smile and smoked salmon bruschetta to each guest. Society's finest kissed the air near each other's cheeks. Hundreds of tables ringed the dance floor. Above her, Angela took in more donors glittering on the balcony level. New York's elite sashayed around her, greeting each other famishedly.

Angela smiled back at the server, a small woman with a pixie cut. Ang complimented the purple streaks in her hair. The woman blushed. Angela asked her name as she took some food and a napkin from the platter. The woman told Angela that she looked gorgeous – she wore a champagne-colored gown which brought out her tan. White-gold earrings matched her necklace. Angela's dark hair was pulled back in wavy curls, a single long tress set free.

Ang looked at the number on the little card as she made her way to the table. She knew almost everyone and was quickly introduced to the stray spouse she hadn't met yet. She told them that Joe wasn't feeling well when they asked where he was and then accepted all their sympathies. Ang fell into the rhythm of the conversation – tilting toward each speaker and chuckling dutifully at the punch lines. She was content to listen, to enjoy the meal, to be there, to not really think. She ate a little and laughed a little. As the program began, Angela swiveled in her seat to watch the speakers and presenters.

She and Joe went to the NYC Finest & Bravest Gala fundraiser every year but this year, Joe told her to go without him. He was still recovering at the beach house. Didn't feel up to it yet. She protested at first – *I can't go without you...it's our thing.* But he told her it would be good for her to get out. Take the train to the city. Have fun. He meant, and she knew, that they needed a night apart. *Plus,* he teased her, *now you and your girlfriends can throw off the $200 shoes you spent months picking out and dance barefoot without my commentary.* She left Joe with a pot of beef stew – his favorite – and suggestions for new movies to check out. As she waved and walked out, Joe felt proud to have a wife confident enough to go to a black-tie affair by herself.

Angela loved that the women servers wore ties, not just the men. That would have been the kind of thing she would have leaned over to tell Joe. She glanced at the empty seat next to her, silverware and napkin untouched even though dinner had already been served and cleared. She frowned sweetly into her coffee.

When the fundraiser ended, her friends urged her to come with them to the hotel bar. Their husbands were already there and they had a table. Angela started to say how late it was and she still needed to get on the train. *Oh, come on,* they coaxed. *So much fun* and *you need a night out* and *after-party.*

"Oh, it's an *after-party*? I thought it was just us leaving the ballroom, taking a left, walking through the lobby to the hotel bar and having another drink with the same exact people we just sat with all night. But if it's an *after-party* that I've been invited to, then I must attend this *after-party.*" They shouted like schoolgirls when she agreed to join them.

Angela sat down at the table, her shawl and purse on her lap. The women leaned into the table when they talked about so-and-so or what everyone was wearing. The men laughed about something and drained their glasses. She smirked when she thought of how Joe would have reacted to that: he would have raised his eyebrows at her but smiled at them like he knew or cared about what they were toasting.

One of the husbands got up to get drinks for everyone but Angela stood and told them that this round was on her. She asked what they wanted. The guys were still having whiskey. The girls were through sipping wine and champagne. They wanted dirty martinis: filthy, seawater.

The bar was packed, mostly with people from the fundraiser. To move through the crowd, you waited until an opening emerged or you shimmied sideways between pockets of people or you just plowed through all the shoulders. Patrons crowded the rail two and three deep against the dark granite bar. Some waved twenty-dollar bills to try to get the attention of the bartenders. Many of the men had shed their tuxedo jackets and loosened their bowties. They tried to balance drinks to bring back to wives or girlfriends. The drinks had to be lifted carefully, over more shoulders, and the return route navigated with knee-nudges and 'scuse-mes.

Ang got in line and just stood there in the crowd for a moment. She was happy to let the sounds wash over her. *It's nice not to think about anything for a little while.* She closed her eyes, letting the energy of the room minister to her.

There were two bartenders. They made drinks and took orders with a sense of urgency. One was a big, beefy man with a ponytail. His forehead and neck glistened. He paused often to dab sweat with a handkerchief. He pointed at people when he was ready for their order and he didn't lean forward to hear it despite the din. Never asked anyone to repeat or clarify, either. She realized that he was reading their lips. *This bartender's damn good.*

The other bartender was among the most gorgeous men Angela had ever seen. He wore a black V-neck t-shirt which was pulled nearly taut over his physique. He had bright eyes, dark eyebrows and a fade, parted on the side. He flashed a spokesman's smile over several days' worth of stubble. He leaned in to listen to one customer's order as he poured a G&T for another. Ang figured he was a model making some cash between gigs. A quick glance around the bar confirmed that the other women thought so as well. They held their drinks in front of their faces to peek at him. Then they pointed him out to their friends, who did the same. *This bartender's damn good too.*

Angela ambled forward again. She eventually reached the bar and took out some cash. The guy to her right yelled "hey, buddy" a few times. The beefy bartender looked right through him and pointed at someone else. A few moments later, the spectacular young bartender filled her vision. He leaned in close with a big smile, hands on the bar, to hear what Angela wanted. He wore a wedding band.

"Hey. What can I getcha?" He had a note of hurry in his voice but he wasn't rushed or rushing her. He was even better looking up close.

"Hi. Can I get two whiskeys – one neat, one rocks – and three dirty martinis, please?" The crowd pushed forward and someone bumped her. Then squeezed in next to her.

"Sure thing."

The young man went to prepare Angela's drinks but he was prevented. He turned back around. The woman who had slipped up to the bar alongside Angela now had her hand on top of the bartender's hand. She was up on her toes, bent forward over the bar, cleavage thrust toward him.

Pouty lips murmured "Just a quick vodka soda? I've been waiting so long."

Angela blew out a breath. *Pretty little thing can't wait in line like everyone else? And the boobs? Really?* Her friends back at the table would hear about this. Ang took her in with little sideways glances.

Strapless coal-black mermaid dress, slitted sides. Neckline like an abyss. A single, thin gold chain plunging off her neck and disappearing forever. Hair dark red, like newly poured wine.

When her identity registered, Angela started to gasp but composed herself. Ang felt great in her evening gown but this girl was stunning. For a moment, Angela's hands and arms instinctively covered her waist.

What do I do? Should she call someone? Joe? Should she say something? Should she get out of there? The girl was facing away from her, still flirting with the bartender. Angela heard her father's voice; *Sometimes you're better off taking a walk. But there are certain times where you must stay exactly where you are.*

Angela took a deep breath and waited for the girl to feel her stare. If she had one drink, Angela might have let the whole thing go. If she had three drinks, she might have poured a cocktail on her. But tonight, Angela had two drinks – just right to see what Tori Rowan had to say for herself. Tori had let go of the bartender's hand and noticed Angela, first peripherally and then directly. She turned.

"I don't believe we've met. I'm Angela Brescia."

46

Tori's cheeks turned the color of her hair.

The bartender took advantage of the pause and moved on to other customers.

The younger woman's chin jutted upward. Angela fixed a firm gaze. Tori broke off the look to scan Angela down and up. A slow, satisfied grin developed on Tori's face.

Tori smirked and tilted toward the bartender. He was conferring with the beefy bartender and sharing a laugh at the cash register. "Don't you just hate waiting on a man? I mean, with all your *experience* in life, you must know something about that, right?"

"Hmmm. Yes, that's good, my *experience*. Well, in my *experience*, I've learned it's good to know when men are simply not interested." Angela looked at the bartender then back at Tori. Angela's left hand, glinting, moved to her chest.

Tori was all sweetness and *whatever-do-you mean*?

The vodka soda arrived and Tori sipped it brightly, head down, eyes up. *See.*

"By the way, the bartender is married too."

"Never stopped me before."

Angela laughed a little laugh. "You know what the worst part about all of this is? About your stunt? When the truth comes out, the next girl who really experiences something terrible in her office is going to be less believable. Because of you."

Angela's drinks came. She handed the bartender two fifties without looking at him.

"Mrs. Brescia, it was so nice to meet you," Tori said crisply, eyes already scanning the crowd.

"Tori, you know what, actually, it was really nice to meet you too. Because now that I see you in person, I feel more at peace. I can see that you're a scared little girl who has no clue what she is doing to people's lives. It's all a game to you. I hope someday you realize that. And karma's a bitch. And it's going to come back to you over and over and over again. In the end, it won't be me you'll have to answer to."

The younger woman's eyes tightened as she was about to say something but Angela walked away before she could speak. The drinks she paid for remained on the bar.

Angela's friends cast icy glances at Tori as they left a few minutes later.

It was after two in the morning when Angela let herself into the beach house. She took off her shoes, not her gown, and slid quietly into the big armchair facing the couch where her husband slept. Angela watched him for a long time, his strained breaths a constant allusion to everything they had suffered together. She loved him. Angela pulled the green and yellow quilt over herself and fell asleep watching him sleep.

Back at the after-party, the handsome bartender came over to Tori's group of friends with a drink in his hand.

"Hey there," she turned her chin to him, pleased. *They always come back.*

"Hi. Someone bought this for you on their way out."

"Oh, how nice. Stay and have a drink with me?"

"Thanks, I can't. Just wanted to drop this off."

"Too bad." Her biggest eyes. "Offer is on the table."

He smiled and shook his head. He handed her a shot glass with a ruby-colored drink in it.

"What is it?"

"Jager, schnapps and cranberry. It's called a red-headed slut."

47

SUNDAY, JULY 7

There was no wind so the little notecard hung limply off the telescope. A strong sun died over the water, casting oranges and violets into the emerging twilight. The woods behind the beach house were just starting to fill with hoots and howls. Joe knew that it was still too early to scope the stars – he figured another 40 minutes or so would do it – but the sunsets this time of year were magnificent too. Plus, he joked to himself, he had spent so much time looking at other stars lately that his home star was probably beginning to feel a bit ignored.

From his spot on the deck, he could see into the kitchen. Angela stood at the sink, cutting something for dinner. She *hoosh-ed* a strand of hair away from her face without taking her eyes off her work.

They were doing better. As his health improved, so did their relationship. The emotional recovery was tougher: some nights he woke up to her sobbing. He would draw her into himself, his presence the only consolation he could offer. *I miss them too.*

The bright scene in the sky robbed him of any attempt at organized thought. His mind faded into the colors until, rather abruptly, he prayed the one question he had not yet asked.

"God...why? Why did you allow all this to happen to us?"

A deep sigh overtook him and he crossed his arms behind his head. For a while he was still. When he opened his eyes, he picked up a vivid point in the Heavens. His head tilted to one side. *It's too light out.* And then: *Can't be Mercury or Venus.*

The point grew brighter. And bigger. He reached for his scope but his hands didn't make it.

The orange and violet tendrils in the sky began to move. The streaks of light drifted in opposite directions until they seemed to hesitate and take note of each other. Then each turned and wandered back to the other and when their points touched Joe's heart exploded with joy. The orange and the violet greeted each other like lovers and started to coalesce. The strands swirled around each other, faster and faster, until the light seemed to catch fire. It created a circle of light and color such that Joe understood that he had never seen true light nor true color before. All the while, the point in the sky was churning quicker and nearer and brighter and now it entered the perfect ring formed by the rapidly circling streaks of color.

The bright point, with the burning colors as its honor guard, hovered over the waters of the Atlantic for a moment and then advanced toward the little cove above which Joe sat – enthralled and enraptured. Joe lifted his hands to shield his eyes from the extravagant light and when he felt the brightness vanish he dared to open them. The point and the colors were gone. Juliana sat in the deck chair beside him.

48

Joe knew who it was because it was true and the truth was simple and beautiful. It was her but it was Him. Joe flung himself off his chair and prostrated himself before the Divine, burying his face in the deck's wooden planks.

"My Lord and my God..."

"Did you like the lights?" Juliana asked.

He dared not raise his head or speak in the presence of the Living God.

Juliana hopped off her chair and helped him up. From his knees, Joe was face to face with her. Side-swept black hair and the faint freckles. Skinny arms and skinny legs. She smiled her crooked smile and Joe knew love. She helped him back into his chair and took the one opposite him. Her feet barely scraped the deck.

"Did you like the lights, Joe? I made them for you."

"I did. I did. Yeah. I have never seen anything like that before. Thank you for that."

"My pleasure."

Some logical part of his brain registered that while he was awestruck in the initial moment, Joe was currently not nervous though he was having a real conversation with God. God saw the thought and said "It's because we're so familiar, you and I. We talk every day. We're just talking now. That's why you're not nervous.

"That makes sense."

Juliana motioned toward Angela at the window, still preparing dinner.

"It's getting better with you two. I'm pleased."

"I know, thank G..." Joe stammered. Juliana giggled.

"I wanted to have this conversation with you face-to-face. I want you to know how proud I am of the way you handled yourself during the trials. You did well, Joe."

"Thank you."

"A moment ago, you asked me 'why?' To answer your question, I would like to ask you a question."

Yes, Lord?

"The lights and the colors just now – do you know how that works?" Juliana's face was lively.

"No, I have no idea."

"I love how much you love the universe. I created it for you to enjoy. But please answer me this: were you there when I arranged the galaxies? Where were you when I laid them out in a way that pleased me? My darling one, where were you when the universe was born and the fires of creation spewed forth the primal matter? Did you tell each star – *Here, my child?* Have you ever gone for a stroll from one end of the universe to the other?" Joe understood the reproach but her speech was gentleness itself.

"No, Lord. I haven't."

She turned to the ocean; the dark water was now indistinguishable from the dusk. "And all the fish, Joe? Do you know them? What about the wild things at the bottom of the deep which no one has seen except for me? Do your creatures worship you by their very existence? In what way does a raindrop give you glory? At what time did you first breathe beauty into logic? How did you decide on the mathematics of the universe as an ordering principle? Have you ever felt the texture of the darkness in those places of the cosmos where no light has ever been?"

He shook his head, *no*. He followed her gaze to the woods. "Do the animals call on you when they're hungry, Joe? Do you feed each of them every day? Do you know the complexity of the hippopotamus? The jellyfish? Have you considered how powerful a thunderstorm is? A tsunami? A gamma-ray burst? Tell me about a sandstorm in the desert. The way it first collects itself and then readies itself and then races, almost like it was alive. Does each grain of sand try to find a way to please you? Have you considered each cell in every blade of grass on a wet Scottish countryside?"

He hung his head. She scooted her chair closer to his, so that she could put an arm around his shoulder. It didn't hurt – he felt the wounds there close and heal.

"My beloved son, I chose you for this because you trust me. I am God. Someday you will see everything from my perspective. But until then you can only see things from your perspective. The bottom line, my little one, is that I do not have to answer to you but you to me. I love you and I do not owe you any explanation. I know this is difficult. You think you must present me with masterpieces. Don't good parents delight in receiving scribbles from their children? How much more, then, do I? Just trust me. Trust in my faithfulness without answers or proof or explanations. Believe that I am who I say I am. The Cross is the answer and the response to all suffering."

"Faith is a mystery not a paradox. Do you see the difference, my love? A mystery is dramatic, alluring. It invites you to penetrate its secrets. A mystery is demanding but there is hope of someday seeing the truth of it. And eventually a mystery rewards your perseverance. A paradox is incoherent, meaningless, hopeless. I am mystery, not paradox."

"Believe in my love. I will do the rest. Suffering does not make sense to you: I understand that. Remember, I lived an authentic human life, body and soul. Ask my Son to show you how to find the joy which suffering cannot disturb. Ask my Spirit for the courage to accept with faith that which you don't understand. I see everything from the big picture, the biggest picture. Someday you will see it too and then it will be enough for you. For now, trust me. Am I God only in the good times? Do I cease to exist when evil occurs? Do I cease to exist when you don't hear from me? Endeavor to see everything from my perspective. Try, my love, try. Ask me for everything you can't understand. I will help you. I am who I say I am. I am trustworthy. I am faithful. My beloved child, you are so small – is that such a bad thing?"

Joe understood. Juliana moved to embrace him, a foretaste of the embrace which he was created to enjoy forever.

"I'm sorry, Lord. You're right."

Juliana stood up and cupped his face with her little hands. Their foreheads touched.

"I accepted what you offered me on behalf of Bill. He will be healed. And pray for your other friends, too."

"I will. Thank you, Lord. And thank you so much for...coming as her. I can't tell you how..."

"I know. You're welcome. She can't wait to see you."

Juliana kissed Joe's cheek and whispered something into his ear, that which is unique to one soul only and cannot be known by another.

49

SUNDAY, SEPTEMBER 1

BREAKING NEWS: Jury Clears Brescia; Accuser, Former Partner Indicted

By Millie Keefe
Daily Sentinel reporter

Joseph Brescia, the former CEO of Brescia Global Solutions, was found not guilty on charges of sexual harassment by a Manhattan jury this morning, bringing his lengthy process of vindication to a dramatic conclusion. In a shocking development, city prosecutors brought charges against Larry Denham and Tori Rowan. They contend that Denham, the chairman of the BGS board of directors, and Rowan – who accused him of harassment – colluded to have Brescia ousted and planned to share the profits from the lawsuit.

Brescia, the longtime City Councilman, would not speak to the media outside the courthouse but sources close to him insist he does not plan to countersue the pair. The source says he has fully recovered from several serious health issues and is enjoying retirement.

Check back often for updates as this story develops.

COMMENTS SECTION |YOU MUST BE A REGISTERED USER TO COMMENT, ALL COMMENTS ARE SUBJECT TO THE DAILY SENTINEL SUBMISSION GUIDELINES

Be the first to comment on this story.

50

Father Jack passed through the x-ray machine and collected his briefcase on the other side. The hefty prison guard smiled at the slender priest and signed him in.

"Who you seeing today, Father, the kid from the airport, the quote-unquote terrorist?"

Father Jack smiled at the floor.

"Really? Fifth time this month for you and him. He doesn't seem too sorry for what he tried to do at the airport. He was pretty twisted when we got him. Didn't picture him for the type to speak to a priest."

"You'd be surprised." Father Jack left it there and the guard didn't press.

Another guard led Father Jack into a busy room. He sat down at a bank of visitation booths, the ones with telephones on either side of the glass. A moment later, a young man with shaggy blonde hair was pressed into a seat across from him. They each lifted their phones. Father Jack smiled and the young man did the same.

51

God descended from his satellite office on the 40th floor of 1119 Lexington Avenue and took the long way though his shoes were not in good shape. All the walking will do that. The left sneaker was hanging together with duct tape. God smiled at everyone he saw as he moved through the city. Some people smiled back, some did not. Some offered him a dollar or a cigarette which he graciously thanked them for but did not accept. He entered the park and sat down on a bench. He spent the afternoon enjoying the sun and his children.

A young man in a posh suit - collar unbuttoned, no tie - sat down next to him. He was talking on the phone.

"That's fantastic, Nan. Yeah, I met Dottie briefly at the hospital but I haven't met his friends from the military. He'll be so happy to have everyone together. Alright, great. I'll meet you at their house tonight."

As he hung up the phone, one of the young man's expensive brown loafers bumped into one of God's dirty sneakers, the one that was held together by duct tape.

"Oh, I'm sorry about that sir." The young man had a pleasant way about him.

"Not a problem at all. Sounded like some good news on the phone there."

"Yeah, a friend just got the verdict we were hoping for at the courthouse. We're going to have a party tonight to celebrate."

"Well, that sounds like fun."

"Sir, do we know each other?" Eli was surprised at himself. He didn't think he knew any homeless people but there was something so *familiar* about this man.

"Oh, we may have crossed paths once or twice before," God said with an inviting gleam.

"I'm Eli Morgan," Eli said, extending his hand.

"Felix Culpa," God said, accepting it.

52

TUESDAY, FEBRUARY 20

Snow covered the sand. The frigid wind looked for openings in their coats and around their scarves as soon as they opened the car door. Joe grabbed all of her luggage at once and Angela escorted the young lady into the house.

She was 20. Haitian. Wide-eyed. She moved through the house with Joe and Ang demurely, trying to keep up with them and take in the thousand-and-one details they pointed out. They showed her the kitchen and the living room, and oh, here was her room. Did she like it? Was it big enough? We can make any changes you want, just let us know.

She held her purse in front of her politely and insisted over and over again, as best she could in English, that everything was more than enough and she was so grateful for their generosity.

Joe shifted, trying to balance her suitcases under each arm while asking, "...is it Ros-a-LYNN or Ros-a-LINE? It didn't tell us how to pronounce your name on the paperwork. Or maybe ROSE-uh-line?"

Angela came over to Roseline. "You'll have to excuse my husband and me. We are so excited to finally meet you." Then, to him: "Joe, you probably don't have to carry Roseline's luggage all over the house. You can put them down whenever you're ready, bub."

Roseline tried but failed to suppress a laugh. Ang looked back at Roseline and whispered. "Don't worry, once he calms down he's a pretty terrific guy."

"Thank you, Mrs. Brescia. I am very happy to be here. I am – learning about it all."

"Of course, sweetie. It's your first day here, take your time."

They left her in her room to get settled and rest from the flight. Ang had to take Joe's arm to get him to stop asking Roseline if there was anything else she needed.

A few months ago they decided together that they still wanted to pour out their love on another person in a special way. Maybe it would fill the void a little bit? They thought about adopting but that didn't feel right. They settled on a cultural exchange program. It took months to get everything approved and prepare the beach house for Roseline. The guardians already in residence at the beach house welcomed Roseline's guardian and the three of them began to pray for peace during the moving-in period.

After a jittery first dinner, Joe and Angela and Roseline sat in the living room. They each sipped a glass of Haitian rum from the bottle she brought them as a gift. The conversation lulled and there was a moment shared between the three of them, a collective instinct. This would work. They looked at each other and laughed because they each knew it.

Suddenly, with verve, Joe put his glass down and bounded over to his desk. He rummaged for a second and came back to sit between them. He held up a heavy, faded leather photo album and opened it. Angela's eyes brimmed. Joe turned to Roseline and directed her eyes to the album, to the last page, to a photo of a happy girl with a beautiful, crooked smile.

I am grateful to Most Reverend Leonard Blair, Archbishop of Hartford, for his encouragement and support.

Many folks offered helpful feedback including John Altson, Rev. Melvin Blanchette, Sarah Bruckner, Joe Capone, Mike Cilano, Kathryn Cooper, Stephanie Denyer, Christina Federico, Patti Flynn-Harris, Rev. Jeff Gubbiotti, Ann Kuehl, Brenna Nykaza, Stacy O'Donnell, Ratna Pandey, Bobby Pannell, Nicole Perone, Diana Proto, Suzanne Tanzi, Jennifer X. Williams and Dr. Kevin Rulo, director of the Catholic University of America Writing Center. I am thankful for the faculty and students of the MFA-Creative Writing Program at Albertus Magnus University.

Andrew Calis read the manuscript with enthusiasm and helped me believe in the characters. Every writer should have someone like Julie Cilano to imagine with and see not what is, but what could be. Andrea Hardy cared deeply for the story and taught me how to, as well. Sarah Wallman used brackets to show me that less is more.

The character of Juliana is named for my friend, Julie Neafsey, whose bright light was dimmed but will never be darkened.

Made in the USA
Middletown, DE
08 November 2021